CALL ME CASSANDRA

CALL ME CASSANDRA

MARCIAL GALA

TRANSLATED FROM THE SPANISH BY
ANNA KUSHNER

FARRAR, STRAUS AND GIROUX
NEW YORK

Farrar, Straus and Giroux
120 Broadway, New York 10271

Library of Congress Cataloging-in-Publication Data
Names: Gala, Marcial, 1963– author. | Kushner, Anna, translator.
Title: Call me Cassandra : a novel / Marcial Gala ; translated from the
    Spanish by Anna Kushner.
Other titles: Llámenme Casandra. English
Description: First American edition. | New York : Farrar,
    Straus and Giroux, 2022.
Identifiers: LCCN 2021038618 | ISBN 9780374602017 (hardcover)
Subjects: LCGFT: Novels.
Classification: LCC PQ7390.G24 L5313 2022 | DDC 863/.64—dc23
LC record available at https://lccn.loc.gov/2021038618

Designed by Gretchen Achilles

Our books may be purchased in bulk for promotional,
educational, or business use. Please contact your local bookseller
or the Macmillan Corporate and Premium Sales Department
at 1-800-221-7945, extension 5442, or by email at
MacmillanSpecialMarkets@macmillan.com.

www.fsgbooks.com
www.twitter.com/fsgbooks • www.facebook.com/fsgbooks

1   3   5   7   9   10   8   6   4   2

To Shinere and Shenae Gala Ávila

In memory of Reinaldo Arenas

Like the dead horse
that the tide inflicts upon the shore

—JORGE LUIS BORGES

CALL ME CASSANDRA

'm sitting here, watching the sea.

It's very early, so everyone in the house is still sleeping, but I got up, opened the door, and came out to the balcony. I brought over a chair from the living room to get comfortable. I'm ten years old and it's Sunday, so there's no school, I can spend the morning watching the sea and the morning stretches out to infinity, but then I hear my mother's voice behind me.

"Oh, Rauli, where have you gone off to?"

I feel like I don't want to be this Raúl, I want to be Cassandra, not Raúl. I don't want them to call me Spineless at school, I don't want my mother to call me Rauli, I want to spend a long time watching the sea, until the sea runs out before my eyes and becomes nothing more than a white line that makes my eyes tear up. I'm in Cienfuegos, I'm not yet a little pretend soldier here in Angola where it never rains, the captain still hasn't called me over to his tent to tell me, "Take off your clothes, we're going to play a game you'll like."

The captain is from the eastern part of the island, he drops all his *s*'s when he speaks, and I smile because I'm afraid. I always smile when I'm scared, I can't help it. I smile when we go through the villages and the people see our caravan of war tanks and trucks go by, with their wide-eyed, muddy faces, they watch us with their bare, red-dirt-covered feet, and it seems like they want to say something to me, specifically. I dream that those feet ask me, "What are you doing here?"

But luckily, I am still in my house now and I watch the sea and I think—because I'm very contemplative at the age of ten— I think that I would like to spread my arms and leap and fall on the flagstones, and then Papá and Mamá would cry a lot and José would stop staring at me with that know-it-all face. "Raúl killed himself," they would say at school and this time it would be true and I would be happy, I wouldn't have to steal money again from Mamá to go to the bookstore and buy books and say, "Give me one by Edgar Allan Poe, because they stole mine at school."

"We're out of Poe, but we have Robert Louis Stevenson," the bookseller says. "The book is pretty, with that skull on the cover, but I don't know if it's appropriate for your age."

"It's for Mamá," I say and he puts the book in my hands, looking at me suspiciously.

"Okay, but don't take it to school, because then they'll take it from you. And if anyone asks, it wasn't me who sold it to you . . . Is that clear?"

"Yes," I say, I who can see ghosts.

I peer into the door of my school and there they are, dressed like sailors. My school is very old and used to be a military barracks. It's called Dionisio San Román, after a sailor who died in a September 1957 uprising. I walk back home. I spent my bus money on books and I drag my feet to kick up the dust and then I inhale it. I like the smell of the dust. "Just look at your shoes," my mamá says when I go upstairs and knock on the door to our apartment, which Nancy opens.

"I can see the dead," I tell them, and they don't like it. It's not good to see the dead, it's madness. Now we're all Marxist-Leninists, atheists, and if you see dead people, you must be mad.

"Do you want to be mad?"

"Of course not," I say, and then I hug Nancy and hug my mother. I eat the snack that Nancy puts on the table for me with a smile; I thank her and go to my room to read Stevenson.

I also predict things. My Zeus, I know I will die at nineteen, very far away from Cienfuegos, here in Angola, the captain is going to kill me so that no one finds out about us, I can see it in his eyes, in his mustache, in the way he looks at me.

"Don't let anyone find out about us, okay, Olivia Newton-John?" he says to me when I crouch down to suck him. "I'll kill you, you know, don't you go and ruin my career here, because I'll kill you like a dog, is that clear?"

"Yes," I say, taking the captain's member in my mouth, and then spitting out what he deposits there. I stand up and look out the window, from which the sea is not visible, just the red, hot soil of Angola.

"Why are you up so early?" my mother says behind me. "You're not tired anymore?"

"No, I'm not tired anymore."

But what I can see are the bullets tearing through me, and how I fall so far away from her and from my father, who went out and still hasn't come back. I know where my father is: with the Russian lady, that English teacher we met on the beach at Rancho Luna the day that my mother couldn't come with us because she had a cold, and then my father took us in the old Chevy, and as soon as we got our swimsuits on, my brother and I ran into the warm water, screaming happily, and when we came out, my father was sitting on the sand, talking to a tall blond woman who made a strange contrast to him, because she was refined and had well-manicured hands, while my father's hands are always filthy. He introduced her to us and it turned out the woman was Russian and her name was Lyudmila.

"Like that Gurchenko woman," my father specified.

That Russian woman was very strange, she had almond-shaped eyes, very large, and of a blue so dark they looked black. She gave a kiss to each of us on our wet faces and asked my brother and me what grade we were in and whether we liked to read.

"I want a snack," was my brother's response.

"Fifth grade," I said. "And yes, I like to read."

"Fifth grade?" The Russian woman was surprised. "You seem younger."

"Yeah, he's kind of a midget," my father said and let out a laugh. "He takes after me, but you don't measure a man from his head to the skies, but rather from the skies to his head."

"What about a woman?" the Russian asked, in her pink bikini so tiny that every man walking along the beach turned his head to get a better look, and my father's eyes were so wide it looked like he could fit the whole world inside.

"I want a snack," my brother insisted, and my father, who was naked from the waist up to show off his former-gymnast's muscles, took his wallet from his jeans pocket and held out five pesos to my brother and me.

"Go over to the lunch counter and get whatever you want. Take care of Rauli," he said to my brother, who was already fourteen, which made him think he was a man, and when we're sitting at the lunch counter, he tells me that Russian woman is a whore and that our father is a motherfucker. He says it without bitterness, just like someone repeating a fact. We eat croquettes and have a yogurt, and when we get back to the shore, the tall woman and Papá are still talking, so my brother gives him the change and we head back to the water. I dive in. My Zeus, when I'm at the bottom, I open my eyes and see a fish coming up to me and looking at me and I dream that I am that fish and a boy named Raúl is looking at me, and I feel affected by the transmutation of things and beings, although I don't know that word, I'm just a ten-year-old kid who went to the beach and who finally comes up for air from the deep and sees his father talking to a woman he doesn't know.

"Don't go tattling on me to your mother. Be men," my father says when we get into the Chevy. "If you tell her, I won't bring you to the beach anymore."

"No need to threaten us," my brother says. "Twenty pesos and I won't say a word."

"You think you can blackmail me, you piece of trash?" my father says, but then smiles and hands him the twenty pesos. "You're learning too much."

If I close my eyes, I see him taking the Russian woman to bed and doing something with her body that my ten-year-old self doesn't really understand, but I don't tell my mother because I know she won't like it and she has problems enough already without having to hear about my father and Lyudmila, who later shows up on a very hot day with a plate of potatoes with butter, saying it was a recipe of her grandmother's from Ukraine, and there are smiles all around and she pats my head and looks at José from afar, as if she were scared of him. My brother has a bad rap, the Russian woman respects my brother, my father has whispered to her that he's a difficult kid who's about to get sent to reform school. She likes me better. I know how the Russian woman will die, of a myocardial infarction following a raging case of diabetes, in 2011, just shy of seventy years old, in a suburban neighborhood of Volgograd, formerly Stalingrad. At ten, I can see the Russian woman's death, can see how she opens her mouth asking for water that Sergei, her teenage grandson, doesn't bring her. The Russian woman, in addition to the boiled potatoes with butter, brings something for José and something for me, a Pushkin book that she places in my mother's hand like some kind of great treasure. One thing's for sure: she gets my mother to smile when she flips through the book, because it's in Russian.

"They're not going to understand a word, Svetlana," she tells her, although she is well aware that the Russian woman's name is Lyudmila.

That's how my mother is—there's no one better at fucking with people.

My mother works as the secretary for a boss who makes her feel important, at least more important than my father, a mere auto body repairman, who almost always gets back late to the apartment, tipsy and in overalls so covered in grease and gasoline that she has to go to great lengths to leave them spotless. My father says not to wash them on his account, to just leave them like that, but my mother spends her Sunday mornings soaping and brushing those rough-hewn work clothes.

Atop the living room console are my father's medals from when he was a gymnast, and a picture of him up on the podium of a young socialist athletes' competition.

At lunchtime, the four of us sit at the big dining room table and my mother insists we use all the silverware, but the spoon is all my father needs.

"You're no example for your children," my mother tells him.

"No, I'm not," he admits. "I'm an animal, not like that boss of yours, the *mulato*."

My father hates Ricardo, my mother's boss, who sometimes shows up at the house with a bottle of vodka as a gift of appreciation for his secretary's immense dedication. My mother's eyes well up as she takes the bottle, which she never even tastes. My father drinks the bottle without even thanking her. She's so naïve that she lets herself be introduced to the Russian woman without it even occurring to her that this woman, as refined and distinguished as if she sprang from the pages of a European magazine, would ever notice a brute like my father.

My father is called José Raúl Iriarte Gómez and he was born in Placetas, a small town full of bitter provincial types of Spanish origins who hate themselves for having stayed in town and envy all those who left. My grandfather was called José Ignacio and was a farmworker and an unabashed cockfighter. My grandmother Carmen spoke Galician and grew cabbage and lettuce that she sold all over Placetas. Besides my father, she had four other children, naming each one José, and they all, with the exception of my father, died violently. The oldest two joined the rebel army. José Eduardo was nabbed by a squad of rural guards, en route to the Sierra Maestra, and machine-gunned down on the side of the road. José Roberto was slaughtered in Santa Clara when they took over the armored train. The other two were killed by the same husband who found José Ricardo, the youngest, sleeping with his wife, while the other one, José Felipe, was leaning up against the back wall of the house, playing the guitar, singing a *ranchera* and keeping watch. He couldn't have been a very good lookout, since he didn't hear the approach of the man whom everyone in Placetas knew as Juan the Party Crusher.

"The knife went through José Felipe's kidney," the doctor told my grandmother. "If not for that, he would have survived."

José Ricardo's jugular was slashed by the jealous man, who then stabbed his wife so many times that, according to what my father says when he's drunk and missing his brothers, the guy had a fit and nearly died when he saw the woman he'd killed, so soaked in blood it would turn your stomach. Sometimes my grandparents had nothing to eat but some cornmeal with salt and a little bit of tomato sauce if tomatoes were in season. After the Triumph of the Revolution, my father, who was a teenager by then, focused on sports and mechanics, bought a Chevy from one of those petit bourgeois from Punta Gorda who emigrated as soon as they found out lovely little Cuba was plunging headfirst into communism.

My mother is called Mariela Fonseca Linares and she was born in Cruces, which wasn't yet the grimy town it ended up becoming, but rather a small, prosperous city, with several newspapers and radio stations and an allegedly active cultural life. My mother's mother, Elena Elisa Linares Argüelles, married a white-passing *mulato* named Eduardo Fonseca Escobar, a card-carrying member of the Socialist Party and an attorney, a graduate of one of those colleges in the U.S. South that is just for Blacks. My grandmother's family, sugar plantation owners known throughout the province of Las Villas as *the* Linares, never forgave her that inappropriate love and disinherited her, so my grandmother became a schoolteacher and, with her husband, built a little wooden house that still stands in Cruces. They had twin daughters. My aunt Nancy came out very blond and with blue eyes like me, while my mother was so olive-skinned that at school they called her the Gypsy. They were very close, and when my mother moved to Cienfuegos, her sister moved, too, and lived with us until she got sick with cancer and died. I was eleven years old when Nancy died and my mother was never the same again. Neither was I.

I resembled Nancy so much that I looked more like her son than my mother's.

L et me say it again. If anyone finds out about us, I'll kill you,"
the captain emphasizes. He adjusts his cap in front of the
mirror, places his gun in the holster, and, before going out to inspect the soldiers on guard duty, looks at the portraits, one by one,
of Che, Fidel, Raúl, and Camilo as if they were religious icons.

Then he says to me, "Get the report ready, I need it by
tomorrow."

I have to go to my quarters, get my toothbrush, and rinse out
my mouth. I can't stand the taste of semen on my palate. But I
have to be careful: Carlos, the sergeant from Matanzas, has it in
for me. He swore he'd give me a good beating so I would stop
the nonsense, get with the program, and give him and his goons
the key to the food storehouse. I can't do that. I'm as hungry
as they are, but I can't do that. I have to be careful, if the captain
finds out, he'll send me to jail first, and then back with the other
soldiers, who will keep calling me Marilyn Monroe and other
charming names, and they'll dress me up as a woman on our days
off again and I don't like that, I just don't.

"I'm Cassandra," I once told them. "Cassandra, reborn after

five thousand years, when both Ilios and ancient Greece no longer exist.

"Cassandra, born on an island in the middle of the tropics, that's me. Cassandra, forever condemned to know the future and never be believed," I insisted, because I'd ingested an enormous amount of Angolan aguardiente and it had gone straight to my head.

Carlos said, "No, you're that damned slut Joan of Arc who is going to save us all from the fucking mercenaries from UNITA and South Africa."

The rest of them laughed at the joke. Then he said to me, "Actually, you're Attila's horse. Wherever you go, the grass stops growing."

He knocked me down to the ground with one push, opened his fly, took out his penis, and was about to piss on my face, but Agustín said, "Hey, Carlos, leave him alone, the poor devil, don't take advantage."

Agustín is from Cienfuegos like me, and we spent boot camp in San Miguel together before getting on the ship to Angola. He's a large Black man like Carlos.

"We're just playing with him, he has to toughen up," Carlos says, looking at Agustín with what tries to pass for a smile.

"That's no game," Agustín says. "Stand up, Raúl, you don't have to humiliate yourself like this. Aren't you Cuban? What's wrong with you? Goddammit."

"Well, look who's championing the underdog and standing up for Marilyn Monroe, who would have thought? I didn't expect that from you, *cienfueguero*."

"He's Cuban like the rest of us. If we fuck him up, they'll fuck us all up," Agustín said and held out his hand, which I grabbed to pull myself up.

I was so drunk, it was the first time I'd gotten drunk in my life. Agustín's eyes were tearing up.

"If these Blacks find out what we do to one of our own, they'll rip us to shreds."

The Blacks are the Angolans. The Angolans have eyes in the backs of their heads, they're always there, even when they're not. The Angolans don't like us although they say they do and smile and say that Cuba and Angola are one sole nation and one sole people and Fidel and Agostinho Neto lift their joined hands. They hate us, the captain thinks.

"That's why we have to be very upright with them, very polite, to win them over, so that they understand how generous our cause is, that we've come over here, to butt-fuck-nowhere, to carry out the internationalist legacy, to pay back in spades everything other peoples did for us when we needed it, is that clear?" he says on a very sunny day, standing on a makeshift wooden stage, surrounded by the battalion's top brass.

It is perhaps the third time he's looked at me not like I was just any soldier, but like a lion looks at a lioness, like my tenth-grade literature teacher who took me to his office and loaned me several forbidden novels under the condition that I take good care, very good care, of them, that I cover them with old magazine pages so that no one would see them. "You'll be a writer," he said, however, now I am a soldier for the homeland, very far away from Cienfuegos and its blue sea, very far away from everything, on a continent full of ghosts, the ghosts of kings, dark ghosts of dark wizards, ghosts that recognize me because I've returned to African soil.

"You're Cassandra," the specters say to me as I hear the captain's voice, standing before the battalion, which is standing at attention, listening to him. The same voice, monotonous, emotionally neutral, that whispers "Olivia Newton-John" to me in the night, now says:

"If I find out that you go out to the *quimbo*, you'll see, anyone who goes out without due permission, I'll accuse of being a deserter, so now you know."

They go to the *quimbo* to fornicate.

"The Angolan women fuck for a can of processed meat or sweetened condensed milk, but they're all sick," the captain will say to me later, when he penetrates me for the first time and I yell out from a sharp pain that seems like death. "I like your little white ass better," he'll go on, "it's tender and tight. Tell me about that poet, remember? The one you mentioned the other night, Virgilio something . . ."

"Piñera."

"Is he a fairy just like you? But you should trust me, Rauli, I know you must know which soldiers go off to the *quimbo* to fuck the Black girls, tell me, it really undermines morale and could kill them. The people from the UNITA catch them and carry out an ambush and it's *adiós, cubanito*, and not all that much would be lost, but they are my responsibility."

"I don't know," I say.

"How could you not know?" he says and slaps me hard across the face with his open palm so it doesn't leave a mark. "Tell me or I'll kill you."

He takes out his gun and puts it in my mouth.

"Talk, motherfucker, who's the fucking boss here? If I tell you to talk, you have to do it. Is Carlos one of them?"

I shake my head no, with my eyes full of tears, I deny it. I think that I am not here, in the violent land of Angola, I think that I have not crossed the ocean on a ship full of Russian soldiers that reminded me of Lyudmila, I think that I went to the university, where I study literature and read T. S. Eliot, I think that I am leaning out the balcony again to look at the sea. The gun in my mouth hurts, but I'm not scared, I know I'm not meant to die today. I know what's going to happen today but I can't avoid it, I'm Cassandra and if I tell anyone, they wouldn't believe me. Today, the UNITA will attack the unit with one of those 82 mm mortars that they carry on their shoulders for miles and miles, I know there will be just one casualty, Lieutenant Alfredo Martínez, the battalion's political officer, a recent journalism graduate, whose bad luck it was to end up in a combat unit sent to the Republic of Angola. The mortar will splice Martínez in two, we'll only find half of his body, the other half will have disappeared into the void or been taken by the hyenas. I'll have to write to Martínez's mother, tell her that her son died a hero while fulfilling the most sacred duty of a young internationalist. All of that I know. The revelation comes while the captain is panting behind me, I see it in the mist, I see the dark, golden eye of the young man carrying the mortar on his back, I see the burns and lacerations on his forearms, caused by how hot the mortar's tube becomes when it goes off, because the one on his way is an artillery expert despite his youth, decorated by Jonas Savimbi. I can feel his breath mixing with that of the captain,

I see Martínez and his blue eyes that come from Miramar and his two-bit politician's smile as he speaks to us in the mornings, before our combat preparation, of the attack on Moncada and the "History Will Absolve Me" speech and then of Napoleon Bonaparte and Hannibal and Scipio Africanus and other people who have dared come to Africa to leave their mark, and he gets excited when he can move beyond Fidel and his absurd attack on the barracks and focus on Cleopatra, Mark Antony, and Julius Caesar, those tamers of Blacks, he says, and smiles so it's clear he's joking, since Carlos, Agustín, Roberto, and Ramiro are very Black, and there are also a lot of *mulatos* and light-skinned Blacks in the unit. I think that, if I'd had the courage to beg the captain to remove his penis from my anus, even if he slapped me with one of his short, thick, large-fingered hands that remind me so much of my father's hands, even if he again placed the barrel of the gun in my mouth, I would go warn Martínez. I would go before him, stand at attention, and after a "with your permission, my lieutenant," I would say, "Enjoy life today, drink that bottle of authentic Russian vodka you bought in Luanda and go fuck in the *quimbo*, because this is your last day on earth."

I wouldn't say, "I've come to save you," because I know that each of our fates is permanently fixed in the sky with no way out, and so, when I had just turned seventeen, high school under my belt and college literature studies awaiting me, and I was called by the medical commission of the Military Committee and had to undress, go from doctor to doctor, show my penis and my anus and sit on a chair where many naked young people before me had set their asses, and when a colonel who looked Asian and noticed my obvious femininity asked me if I was homosexual,

I firmly shook my head, and not only out of fear of the consequences, but also because I knew my fate was to be here in Angola and die in the Old World where everything began, my Zeus, where I was first Cassandra such a long time ago. At twelve at night, that little soldier from the UNITA will come within five hundred yards of the unit and then set up the mortar.

He wasn't always like this," my mother tells Lyudmila, because I snuck out of school again and the Russian woman went to look for me on the promenade in her blue Lada and saw me sitting, watching the sea, and called me over with her mouth full of *r*'s, "Raurito."

Then she got out of her car and sat down next to me and talked to me about the world and it's strange because she's put my hand in hers and I feel close to that infamous Russian woman who wants to take my dad away from us and now tells me, "Let's go back, they're very worried," and I get into the car and I return and I'm eleven years old already and they're waiting for me in the living room, my brother José and my dad, and they say, "Happy birthday, Raulito," and I smile because it's my birthday and the Russian woman acts like some kind of hero because she managed to bring me back home, all in one piece, without a hair on my head out of place.

"Why didn't you go to school?" my father asks.

"It's my birthday."

"Duty first," he says and smiles.

My father doesn't like me, I can tell by his baleful gestures, his tired glances, by the clumsy way he pats my head. My father knows I know his secret, he doesn't know how I know it, but he knows. My mother knows it, too, my mother shows off her very white teeth and says, "Happy birthday, Raulito."

My mother is wearing a flowered dress, it's a Russian dress, my mother's sandals are also Russian and she herself looks Russian since she went blond without realizing she's imitating Lyudmila, it's all very strange. Even I look more Russian than Cuban because I'm very blond, too white for the sun of the tropics, and too feminine.

"You remind me of Julien Sorel," the Russian woman says without my catching the reference. "You look like a little nineteenth-century French boy, so delicate."

Lyudmila strokes my face. My brother José gives her a vicious look. My brother José looks at everyone viciously, he's like that, he'll die at thirty-five in a motorcycle accident, very far away from here, in Nebraska, so my parents will outlive both of us, but they don't know it yet. We all look so happy and young, and the Russian woman has brought me a gift, Tolstoy's *War and Peace*.

saw Oyá of the seven skirts fight Anubis for Martínez's soul until the soul split in two and one half went off to the Nile while the other half went to the falls of Lake Victoria. But Martínez's body remained there on the perimeter, very close to our quarters. He was missing his legs and when morning came, they were still missing. The group that went to hunt down the one who threw the mortar came back. The captain was in front, his eyes tearing up.

"They got us, dammit, if it wasn't for the South Africans getting closer, I would go and put a bullet through every one of those fucking Blacks," the captain said and Martínez wasn't there to tell him it wasn't appropriate to talk like that, that it affected the troop's morale. The troop that, with Gilberto, Ernesto, Amado, Sergio, and Raymundo, the five lieutenants and company commanding officers at the head, had its rifles ready as if from every dark corner, behind every hill or tree, a soldier with a mortar was about to race out and aim his projectiles at us. Not me, I don't have to go get my rifle, I'm the unit's precious jewel, I draft my reports and also dispatches and obituaries. My uniform is bright green, almost as I received it in Cuba, the captain likes for me to look good. If it were up to him, he would even let me grow my hair long, almost to my shoulders, so that I would really look like a girl, but even he doesn't dare to go that far, they could execute us if they found out what we do, or rather, what he does to me, because the captain undresses me without my asking him to, forces me down on my knees to suck him off, and then he penetrates me in one thrust and calls me dirty ass and broken ass and says I look a lot like her, his beloved wife who is in Cuba and who hopes he returns so she can get pregnant and build a little house in Gibara, the most beautiful town in Holguín, which has a promenade alongside the sea that looks like the one in Cienfuegos, although not as big. He says all of this to me as he penetrates me and delays reaching orgasm because he's not focused. At heart, he hates me, although I am his little jewel.

I don't like being the captain's little jewel.

"You're the captain's little whore, huh?" Carlos whispers when we meet in the mess hall.

He's so close to me that I can feel his breath on my ear.

"You can't be trusted, but don't say anything about me, fag, 'cause a bullet can get away from anyone."

I nod my head. He knows I'm strange, that's why he treats me like this. Carlos is kind of a witch. He's on the land of his ancestors, his senses are heightened, and he knows that he and I are in tune with each other. He is my immediate commander because I was assigned to his infantry squad. The first time he saw me, he laughed.

"They're scraping the bottom of the barrel, you'll never be a soldier, you're cannon fodder . . . unless you know karate. Do you know karate?"

"No," I said to him and he looked at me with such concentrated disgust that it was practically love.

"Let's find out," he said, "throw a punch at me."

I pressed my lips together and shook my head.

We had just arrived in Luanda in a large ZIL war truck, Agustín, Johnny the Rocker, and I, it was Saturday, and I was meeting Carlos Valdivia, my sergeant, who wanted to show me that I was no soldier.

"If you don't do it, I'll be the one punching you," he said then, and the other recruits laughed.

Naked from the waist up, they had been playing volleyball, soccer, and baseball up until that moment. The captain wasn't around. No officer was. The soldiers stopped playing and started surrounding us. No one said, *Hey, guys, stop it.* No one wanted to get into a fistfight with Sergeant Carlos Valdivia, whose super-sculpted arm muscles and broken nose revealed that he had once been a boxer.

"I don't know you," I said at last, "I'm a soldier for the homeland, I came because of Sara González and her song about the heroes . . . *Y que viven allí / donde haya un hombre presto a luchar / a continuar.*"

"Are you making fun of me?" Carlos asked, but then he started laughing. "We've got a singer."

Angola's red earth is full of ghosts.

"Angola's witches and witchcraft are all dead gods," the captain says. "We came here to sow Marxism-Leninism and to end colonial exploitation."

He says it while he watches a company of young FAPLA soldiers, who come to train with us. They barely understand Spanish but they nod their heads, although they know, like I do, that the gods are alive. Nothing that was ever alive can die, those young people know.

wouldn't have wanted for it to be so crude, I would have wanted
my soul to soar higher, and for us to have told each other things
we never said, when you looked at me with those eyes in which
there glowed a secret light that I barely understood.

"Why are you going?" Roberto asked me as we put on our
makeup in front of the mirror at his house.

"It's my duty to the homeland."

"Never mind duty, tell them you're a fairy," he said to me
while I applied my eyeliner.

"Stay with me, Rauli, please, you're my only friend," he said
while he filled in my lips, but there was no way, the leopard's eyes
were already inside of me, I was part of the leopard, over there on
the red earth of Cunene.

"Now that my parents left, like scum, I'm so alone, Rauli, I
need you, what's a girl like me going to do around here, Rauli,
don't go, please . . . What kind of a soldier are you? Not even a
tin soldier, please!"

"I have to go . . . I don't want to be Raúl, or Nancy," I said,
but I didn't tell him that I knew I was going to die, I didn't tell

him that. What for? It's better to leave him full of hope. Let him think there's some future to our friendship.

I don't want to be Raúl, I always knew that, ever since I was a child, I knew. I am not Raúl because I am Cassandra and Priam's blood runs through my veins. The gods told me so.

"You're only here in passing, you will again cross the Hellespont and will again sacrifice to us a long-horned ox," Athena told me and I watched her feet shod in golden sandals making a subtle trail, invisible to everyone else, inside the private Spanish and literature room, when the teacher came over to put his hand on my shoulder and say I was beautiful, almost like a girl.

Athena is behind the teacher with a smile in her owl's eyes and she speaks to me in an ancient language that I understand very well.

"You must return to the ancient world," she tells me. "Over there in the land of the hirsute Ethiopian, your time in this era comes to an end."

Her voice in my head is as loud as the thunder of a chariot led by a hundred fiery horses. The teacher feels me go rigid under his hands and lets go.

"You're cold, Raulito, is something wrong?"

I go home. I'm fourteen years old and I remain ill, lying in bed, waiting for Athena to come back, to come from Mount Olympus with her light feet to tell me the secrets of a time that has already passed.

DOWN WITH SCUM says a sign in front of Roberto's door. DOWN WITH SCUM says a sign in front of the door of the home of my best friend, who didn't go to school this afternoon because his parents are packing their suitcases.

Roberto hasn't done his military service yet so he won't be able to go with them.

"They're stateless, traitors of the Homeland and the Revolution that has given them everything," says our geography teacher, who is also the school's party secretary. The principal is with him. Tall and thin, she clutches a yellow purse as if afraid it could fly away.

"Down with scum!" the principal says. "Remember that eggs are cheap, buy them and throw them, it's time to take a stand and you're no longer children. It's time to take a stand! Down with scum!"

"Down with scum!" we students and the teachers yell in unison.

"Piff, paff, out with the riffraff!" the principal shouts.

"Piff, paff, out with the riffraff!" we all shout.

She says, "If you don't jump, you're a traitor!"

And we repeat, "If you don't jump, you're a traitor!"

We all jump at once, the whole school in the air for a second that becomes an eternity, but as soon as our feet touch the ground, the principal shouts, "If you're Black and you depart, the Ku Klux Klan's gonna tear you apart!"

"If you're Black and you depart, the Ku Klux Klan's gonna tear you apart!"

It rains lightly, just barely. The principal of Rafael Espinosa Middle School, in the center of that void that is Cienfuegos, finishes by saying in a high-pitched voice, "Class is over today. You can go condemn that engineer Ortiz who betrayed the revolution that gave him everything . . . Down with scum!"

Engineer Ortiz's son is my only friend, nevertheless, I go with everyone else, I walk along the sidewalk with the others and shout with the others and with the others, I buy discounted eggs. What I'm doing is wrong, I know it, it's wrong to have been reborn, it's wrong to be again. I'm going to throw eggs at the family of my best friend, at a gray door that won't open. They haven't left the house in three days. Spineless Raúl is going to throw eggs at his only friend. I am not him, I am Cassandra, who does have a spine, made up of so many bones that no one else sees. The Russian woman sees me going to throw eggs at Roberto, she gets out of her Lada and calls me over.

"Raúl, come here."

I break off from my classmates and cross the street.

"Where are you going, Rauri?" she says after seeing the bag of eggs in my hand. "That's not right, Rauri, you don't build socialism by throwing eggs."

So how do you build it, I want to ask her, but I don't, I just keep staring at her eyes, which are a very dark blue.

"Did you read the book?" she asks there, in the middle of the street, while my classmates shout, "Down with scum, down with scum!"

The Russian woman has a bit of scum in her, she's wearing tight jeans now when it's dangerous to go around in tight jeans, it's not good for anyone to be seen with the Russian woman, for me or still less for my teachers, who look behind them as they walk, and the leader of my Middle School Students' Federation detachment also looks back as if to say, "What does this one want from Spineless Raulito? Could she be a CIA agent?"

"Did you like it?" the Russian woman insists.

"Yes, Svetlana."

"You know very well that my name is Lyudmila. We've spent years doing this, you have to learn to accept me, Rauri . . . You don't have to go, it's not compulsory for you to go."

"I know, I want to go."

You're a real hero," my mother says when I'm already in the
unit known as "*la Previa*," where newbie soldiers spend six
weeks of intensive military training and you learn to use a rifle,
to march, and to obey.

My mother looks at me, visibly moved.

"You're a man now," she says and hugs me and cries a little.

The Russian woman and Papá have also come. Soon we're off
to Loma Blanca where they do the last medical checks, give you
one set of civilian clothes and a dog tag with your name engraved
on it so that you can die with the certainty that you'll be identi-
fied, and then send you off to the ship and to Angola. Lyudmila
has brought me bread she baked herself, Papá a bottle of Bulgarian wine, and Mamá a pot of arroz con pollo. I call over Agustín to
share the food with me. He refuses at first, but finally comes over.

"What a beautiful boy," the Russian woman says and Papá
gives her a serious look.

"You shouldn't have brought Svetlana," Mamá says without
looking at her. "I don't know what she's doing here, he's not
her son."

"Excuse me, Mariela, but no one brought me here," the Russian woman says. "I came on my own, I have two feet."

"Nobody's talking to you, Svetlana," my mother says.

"These are my last days in Cuba," I say. "I'd like to enjoy them in peace."

"Yes," my mamá says. "But certain people don't know their place, it seems that over there in Siberia, they don't teach them very well, shall we say . . ."

"Please, Mariela, that's enough," my father says. "The boy is leaving us and you . . ."

"In three weeks, we'll be sailing to Angola," Agustín interrupts as he sits between my papá and me, unable to take his eyes off the arroz con pollo.

We're the only ones from Cienfuegos in the whole preparatory unit. The others are from Villa Clara, Camagüey, Sancti Spíritus. There are even two guys from Granma.

I'm almost in Angola already, going to meet my death. Apollo is taking me, he won't let Athena protect me. I am at the heels of the sandals of this god, who appears to me in dreams as soon as I lie down in the soldiers' hammocks. He is Black, tall, and athletic and says he is called Shango. He looks at me with dark brown eyes and says to me, "Oh, daughter of Priam, I have found you and nothing can protect you from my rage."

I'm sitting in front of my father, whose arm is slung over the Russian woman's shoulders and who looks at me with a smile, perhaps of compassion. I can't help knowing how my father and my mother will die, as well as my brother, who is over there in Cienfuegos getting drunk on ninety-proof alcohol cut with orange juice while listening to Pink Floyd. I know how they will die, long after I die, and my eyes fill up with tears and I say:

"There is, mother, a place in the world called Paris. A very big place and far off and once again big."

"César Vallejo," says Lyudmila, who knows it all, and then she tells me that when I return she's going to give me a very beautiful book by a writer I don't know and I'm going to like it as much as *War and Peace*.

"Mikhail Bulgakov is his name."

Then my mamá serves the arroz con pollo but doesn't offer any to the Russian woman, who moves away seriously and lights a cigarette, and my father also gets up and goes with her, so that leaves Agustín, my mother, and me sitting on the benches, next to the rose bushes.

"I don't know how he could have brought that whore," my mother whispers and I want to tell her not to think about Lyudmila, to think about me, to take a good look at me because she's seeing me for the last time in her life, soon I will be ashes and nothing will make sense since I'll be Cassandra again, and if we meet each other again in another era, she won't recognize me. I am tempted to tell her, but I don't do it, I leave. They take me to Angola, I'm just another tin soldier, I'm cannon fodder.

I

t's raining again. It rains on the earth of Angola and turns everything the color of the eyes of the leopard the captain killed because it had entered the village on the hunt for a calf. Martínez's eyes also look like the leopard's. I must write a letter in which I say that Lieutenant Alfredo Martínez fell while fulfilling the most sacred duty for a young Cuban, the internationalist duty. I must write this to a mother who will receive the words over there in Miramar and will go mute as she looks at this sheet of yellowing paper. I must write it this very day so that the captain, my captain, can sign it just prior to penetrating me, just prior to submerging himself in Cassandra like someone arriving safely at port.

Here in Africa, the gods don't disguise themselves. I see Apollo, I see him with his bow and arrows, smug in his glory, I see him walking next to me when we enter the bush, rifles at the ready. I will soon be dead, Apollo knows it.

I was born with my eyes wide open, I stole my mother's clothes, I put on makeup and wanted to look like my aunt Nancy, who was very much alive then and going out with a Bulgarian engineer who spoke Spanish with a very funny inflection and would visit us with a bottle of Moldavian wine under his arm for my parents and some chocolates for me and for my brother, and would then leave with my aunt, kissing us first before leaving, and my father would mutter that Nancy was the odd duck of the family and that she was going to freeze to death over there in Sofia, and she'd deserve it, off-kilter as she was.

"I wanted to introduce her to a friend of mine, a brilliant mechanic, who had a car and everything, and she chose this effeminate little Bulgarian instead."

"Oh, shut up, José Raúl," my mother would say. "Leave my sister alone, I don't mess with your family."

When I was alone with my mother, I would go into my aunt's room, open the drawers of her wardrobe, that always smelled somewhat perfumey and unexplored, and would look for a blouse I could wear as a dress, then I would stand in front of the mirror, put on makeup, and, carefully, go over to the room I shared with my brother and there, seated with my legs crossed in the rocking chair my father had made especially for me, I would wait for my mother to leave her domestic tasks aside to find out why everything was so quiet.

"But Rauli . . ."

"I want to be Aunt Nancy."

"Take all that off quickly, please, you're going to be an actor, and yes, you are the spitting image of Nancy with that same blond hair and those eyes that are so blue, but hurry up, my boy . . . get to doing something useful, play cops and robbers, come on, your brother is about to come home and I don't want him to see you like that, he might tell your father, and you know how he is, that brute."

My father is at the sugar harvest, the "ten million ton" harvest that I know won't come to pass, they're not going to get anywhere near that many millions, of tons of sugar or anything. I know because I am Cassandra. My brother is twelve years old and is always enraged over something of which my mother and I are ignorant. His rage is noticeable even in the way that he looks at everything, with concentrated and visceral hate. I always thought my brother would end up killing the family, that one day we would turn up stabbed in our beds, I thought it until I had the revelation about how we would all die and that I would die here in Africa, on the border with the Old World. In a way, it would be a return to Ilios, where the old gods would be waiting for me and also the ghosts of my lovers Agamemnon and Ajax, who should have never torn me away from the statue of Athena when I wrapped myself around her, Ajax who forcefully took what I would have happily given him and who appeared to me in the distance as soon as I disembarked here in Angola, hazy beneath the light of Africa, to tell me:

"Oh, Cassandra, daughter of Priam, you've returned."

At four years old, I had my first revelation. I was playing in the yard and then I saw how the lines of the checkerboard floor of my room did not cross, all became instead the waves of a river that led nowhere. The river was the Acheron, I know that now, and out of nowhere, navigating that river, the oldest ship in the world appeared, steered by a ferryman with an endless beard who lifted his hand full of swallows and asked me, "Cassandra, do you have the obol?"

I opened my mouth and Charon took the coin that someone had left on my tongue.

Later, on a very hot afternoon, someone showed up when the other kids in the preschool had surrounded me and were shouting "ladybird," she smiled and I knew she was a goddess because only a goddess could, with the mere blowing of her lips, scatter the children, turning them into dogs for a minute and making them flee with their tails between their legs. Twenty children marked for a psychologist, thanks to the magic of the goddess who bent over, patted my head, and told me that in Cuba they called her Obatalá.

"But I'm Athena, and I was born dancing a warrior's dance . . ."

"Athena?"

"Take a good look at me, oh, Cassandra, don't you remember?"

"I'm Raúl."

"No, you are Cassandra, lucid in divinations, go and tell your mother to buy *The Iliad* for you and you will understand and know who I am, and above all, you will know who *you* are, tell her that they published it in a Cuban edition and that the book is in all the bookstores and that there's also the book about my beloved Odysseus, but to start with *The Iliad*."

At the mention of Odysseus's name, I wanted to throw up, I felt such great aversion that I had to bring my hands to my mouth and close my eyes. When I opened them, the goddess had gone and I was alone in the schoolyard and the teacher was running toward me.

"What did you do to them?" the teacher asked me, shouting.

"Nothing, ma'am, nothing."

"Something happened. What was it?"

"I don't know, ma'am . . . we were playing and . . ."

"Tomorrow, bring your mother in, tell her I need to talk to her."

The teacher knows I'm strange.

"You have to take him to a psychologist," she tells my mother. "He's very effeminate and a crybaby. If he goes on like this, he'll have a lot of problems."

"You don't know what you're talking about," my mother yells at her. "My son is very macho, yes, ma'am, make no mistake, his father's brothers are martyrs who fought in the Sierra Maestra and his father was a national gymnastics champion."

"I'm just saying . . ."

"I don't care what you have to say," my mother says and then she takes me by the hand and walks so quickly that I can barely keep up with her.

"Let's go straight home so you can explain to me what happened, Rauli."

We had to wait for a bus for over twenty minutes and that whole time, my mother, sitting next to me in the bus shelter, never stopped tapping her foot in rage.

"I'm telling you, that woman is going to hear it from me . . . I'm going to change you to another school, but first, I'm going to grab her by the hair and give her a beating . . . That will make her remember me for as long as she lives . . . I'm a decent person, but when my Black side comes out, I'm not forgiving."

Then the bus came and my mother, sitting next to me as I watched the city parade by my window, maintained a tenacious, ferocious silence. We got out and are already in the living room and my mamá is sitting in the rocking chair in front of me, while

I'm on the sofa, and she rocks violently. I see how my mother's small feet lift up and fall back down on the checkerboard floor, which luckily is still a checkerboard today, and not a river of turbulent waters.

"Talk," my mother says.

"A woman in blue and white appeared to me and told me that you should buy me *The Iliad*."

"*The Iliad*? What woman was this? Where did she come from? Is she a teacher?"

Then I can't help letting the word *goddess* fill my mouth and it insists on falling onto the checkerboard floor and breaking on that afternoon when my mother and I are seated face-to-face looking at each other.

"A goddess? You mean a madwoman. Gods don't exist, my child, now we're all Marxist-Leninists, and the gods don't exist, is that clear . . . ? Is that clear?"

"Yes, Mamá."

Now the kids at school look at me in fear, some burst out in tears at the mere sight of me, then they move me to another school. Now I'm at Dionisio San Román, which is far away and full of dead people because it used to be a military barracks where there was an uprising against Batista and nearly everyone perished. On Sunday, my mamá takes me to the cathedral so that I can see what religion is, the opium of the people. We take the bus and get out at José Martí Park and we walk to the dark wooden door and I see the old women going inside to pray, old women who don't look at my mamá or at me and who "shrink fearfully before the power of the new truth," my mother says. This is not the house of the goddess, I think, but I don't say anything, I've had enough for today, so I nod my head and say, "Let's go buy the book."

"What book?"

"*The Iliad.*"

"Well, that can't happen, you have more than enough with the books you already have," she says and I burst out crying so hard that it was as if the entire park went still, as if my shouting could stop the birds in the air. When I cry like that, the whole world stops to watch. My mother fears that ancestral cry.

"You hush, you're too big now to be crying, come on, let's go, I'll buy you the book. If you calm down, of course."

We go to the bookstore.

My mother takes me by the hand as if I'm going to fly away.

"Good afternoon, *compañero*, do you have *The Iliad*?"

"What?" the salesperson asks, but my mother has spoken so quietly that she can't even hear herself.

"My mamá wants to know if you happen to have *The Iliad*?" I intervene and the salesperson looks at me from above, surprised by my shrill voice and the very un-Cuban way that consonants and vowels emerge from my mouth, as if he were afraid that he would miss one.

"It came in three days ago," he says and puts the bulky orange book in my mother's hands. "That's two pesos, fifty."

"How expensive," my mother says and reaches into her purse.

Sing, O goddess, the anger of Achilles, son of Peleus!

I have *The Iliad.* I go to my room.

"What's that? The Bible?" asks my brother, who snatches the

book away from me before I can stop him and then calmly pages through it. "Poetry? You're going to end up like José Martí, bald and with a bullet through the head."

He's naked, except for the bathing suit he wears to play water polo. He sits on his bed, which is just above mine, and scratches his feet with his left hand while he holds the open book with his right hand and begins to read out loud. I look at him, mouth agape, watchful as a dog. I'm afraid he'll take the book and toss it out the window. From the kitchen, we can hear my mamá singing as she makes dinner.

"Oh qué será, que será / Que no tiene remedio y no lo tendrá . . ."

Aunt Nancy is sick already and her Bulgarian boyfriend has left her. Now she's going out with a long-haired Romanian who's kind of a cad and says he's a Gypsy and hates the Czechs because he studied in Prague and they discriminated against him because he looked Cuban:

"I was at Kafka's house . . . Kafka had a hard time, too, because those Czechs are dogs, and he liked whores, he would go from brothel to brothel," I hear him saying from my room as soon as he comes in with Nancy, after the introductions.

My aunt kisses her sister, who goes to make the coffee, and then sits down with Emilio Ionesco, that's the Romanian's name, on the sofa, and they keep talking about Prague and literature. I hear Nancy's gurgling laughter while the Romanian keeps trying to make a good impression on my mother.

"Nancy is sick," José tells me suddenly as he returns the book to me, he says it with tears in his eyes because he also loves my aunt.

My brother should take a shower, his feet stink so badly I

don't think I'll be able to sleep, so I turn off the light, get under the sheet, and use a flashlight to start reading. It's only six in the evening, at eight my mother will call us to dinner, and when I go in, I'll force my brother to take a shower. "To get rid of that chlorine stink you brought from the pool."

It's hard for my mother to recognize that her favorite son's feet smell putrid. I already showered, but I'll shower again, I like being clean and my mother knows it. I also like to stand in front of the mirror and pretend I'm another person.

I read about Priam, about Hecuba, about my brothers in Ilios and about those infamous Achaeans: Menelaus, Agamemnon, Patroclus, the two Ajaxes, and Odysseus, ever scheming, the worst of the lot, worse still than Achilles with the homicidal hands. I read and there's a horrific downpour outside, it's almost cerebral, as if it were raining inside my head. From the living room come the voices of the Romanian, Nancy, and my mother. My father isn't home. My father went out very early to fish for crabs. I like it when my father shows up with a bag full of dead crabs and my mother cooks them extra spicy, although sometimes my father arrives with a live crab and the animal scurries amid the living room furniture and seems to look at me with its pendulous eyes and my father wants my brother to prove he's already a man.

"Take it carefully, José—don't let it get you with one of its pincers because, baby, you'll see stars—then give it to Raulito."

I tremble at the anticipation of taking the crab in my hands. I go to my room and shut the door. From the living room comes my father's laughter, a hoarse cackle that is drawn out until it fades into nothing. I hear my brother say I am effeminate, he says it real loud so I'll hear it.

"Raúl is a fag."

"Shut your mouth, dammit, I don't want to hear you talking about your brother like that again, he's only seven years old . . . Raulito, come here, don't make me come and look for you!" my father says.

My father's hands are big and porous, too big for someone with such a small body. My father's boss at the auto body shop, where he has worked as long as I've known him, is Black. My father doesn't like being ordered around by a Black man, even if he is an engineer while my father's a simple mechanic, he says so every once in a while.

"These people have gotten too big for their britches," he says and looks at my mother before spitting out: "It's a good thing your people landed on the right side of the fence."

The right side of the fence is his side, with the very white people, while my mother's darker skin tone makes it easy to tell she has Black blood running through her veins. My maternal grandfather didn't accept my father: a mere dull-witted mechanic with long hair and a tendency to drink too much. I don't know what Lyudmila the Russian is going to see in my father when they meet. I suppose she'll be bewitched by that scruffy gangster air about him that has always been his signature. "I'm a pimp and a killer and a big shot, that's me!" was my father's preferred slogan, which he usually said when he came home very late, stumbling around the living room.

"I explode sometimes," he would say later, and I imagined him splayed out in shards across the checkerboard floor of the living room that would soon turn into a sea of vertical lines going nowhere. I have to leave my room before my father comes to look for me, I have to stand in front of him with my hands behind my back and look him in the eye. My father can't stand for his sons to talk to him while looking at the floor or waving their hands around, his sons must show him respect. I am half of my father's sons and I have to look into his blue eyes where there is always a hint of fear, as if my father were afraid of finding out who I am.

"Leave him be, José, he's just a child," my aunt Nancy says and gives me an encouraging smile.

The three blonds in the house are Nancy, my father, and me, the three who have blue eyes, and that resemblance, instead of making us closer, drives us apart. The scene remains fixed in my memory, my Zeus, I see myself in the living room, where there's a crustacean in the middle just as fearful as I am, as I run and hug my mother's legs, while my father looks at my aunt bitterly.

"Nancy Fonseca, let me explain something to you: a man is macho from the day he's born."

"Says who?" my aunt challenges him in a low voice. "Did you happen to learn that fixing engines? I didn't know you could learn pedagogy under a truck."

"I learned it on the streets, ever since I was this big." My father almost crouches down and holds his hand very close to the floor. "And if this son of mine has to learn it, too, so should everyone who lives under my roof."

"This house isn't just yours," my mother interrupts on behalf of her sister, who is already showing the signs of her illness, she looks worn out, with bags under her eyes, thin-skinned and bony, her hair messy and a book always in her hands. I know she's going to die, anyone can tell. The Romanian boyfriend will be the last adult male to desire that body and hold it tight. The other men in Nancy's life will be the doctors in Havana's oncology center, where she'll be admitted and leave only when she dies. I won't see her die, my mother will spend the last months of her sister's life at the hospital, and when she returns, she will have changed so much that we won't recognize her. While my mother cares for her dying sister, my father will be running around with the Russian woman. They will become so intimate that by the time my mother returns, she will be no more than an outsider, someone who was no longer expected to come back. My father will come home smelling like the Russian woman, will sit down at the table smelling like the Russian woman, will say a word and sound like one of the Tolstoy characters I got to know through *War and Peace*. We're going to miss Nancy but we're going to miss her in different ways, my brother will masturbate thinking about that beautiful aunt he'll never see again, and my father will blame her for the failure of his marriage because he married the wrong sister. My mother and I will have to revive her in order to keep on living.

Now that Nancy isn't here, I will have to be Nancy for my mother.

It kills me to see you sad / your sorrowful face, sweet love of mine . . . It was my aunt Nancy's favorite song.

"Come on, get the crab," my father says, and I see the crustacean dragging itself with its raised pincers, ready to attack, scattering yellow sand across the living room my mother cleans so diligently. The crab is also afraid. I don't want to touch it and I burst out crying, then I let out a scream almost as loud as the one Achilles let out when Patroclus died.

"Leave him alone," my mother says. "The neighbors will come knock on the door."

"He has to learn to be a man," my father says.

I don't learn to be a man. I dress up in Nancy's clothes, I take one of her Populares-brand cigarettes and pretend I'm smoking. I smoke in front of the mirror. The plumes of smoke are actually incense that I place before the statue of Athena over there in Ilios. As a votive offering, I leave a handcrafted bronze amphora vase. Then I slash the throat of a very white lamb and ask the goddess not to allow the Achaeans in my city, to preserve Hector's life above all, I ask this of the goddess under the gray, fly-infested skies of Ilios.

M arilyn Monroe!" Carlos shouts at me because he wanted a
cigarette from me, and I didn't give him one since I don't
have any, I don't smoke.

"You think you're so smart, Marilyn Monroe," he says then,
"but I'm your sergeant, and if I ask you for a cigarette, you have
to have one. What are you thinking, you fucking whore? Go on
and get one."

"I can sing another Sara González song for you," I whisper,
which makes him shout at me to speak louder, *are you retarded
or what?*

"I can sing like Sara González for you."

"Don't get smart with me!" Carlos shouts. "I want a cigarette, goddammit!"

I look at the other soldiers. At Matías, who has removed his
military shirt and sits on a rock, smoking. At Fermín, who is also
smoking, not very far from Matías. At Rogelio Isidrón, the fat
one, perhaps the weakest one after me, who avoids looking at us
as if afraid that Carlos, with that characteristic unpredictability
of his, will forget about me, turn to him, and shout, "I don't want

any fatties in my squad, what's wrong with you? Go on a diet, go running, don't make me repeat myself!"

Rogelio Isidrón draws naked women for everyone else to masturbate to. The drawings come out with a certain realistic element very much to the other soldiers' liking, so he's more or less accepted. I am not accepted. There's no officer nearby, they're training the Angolan soldiers, so Carlos can go off at will. Even Agustín isn't around: he's in our quarters, writing a letter to his girlfriend. Agustín's girlfriend is called Teresa and I met her in Cuba, when we were in boot camp together. She's a tall, light-skinned *mulata*, the sister of that soldier who deserted, who was renamed Militiawoman and beaten so badly for refusing to go to Angola. I didn't refuse to go to Angola. I'm here, with Carlos breathing on my face and shouting at me, "A cigarette, Marilyn Monroe!"

I'm very still, I barely breathe, I only look him in the eye. I know how he will die, at seventy years old, of an aneurysm, in Matanzas where he was born, but knowing this is useless to me. I'm not yet the captain's beautiful wife, he doesn't yet dress me in that expensive women's clothing he brings back from the mansions of Luanda's colonists, I don't yet paint my lips red and my lashes bluish-black, regardless, this Carlos already thinks he knows that I am Marilyn Monroe, but I am Cassandra.

"I don't have any, I don't smoke."

"Oh, the little girl doesn't have cigarettes. Well, you have to have cigarettes here," Carlos says and crouches down.

Amaury, close by him, big and fat, smiles as he watches Carlos scooping up a big fistful of yellow dirt.

He stands up again.

"Attention, soldier! Remove your hat. If you move, I'll kill you, you hear? Is that clear?"

I stand at attention, as straight as a column in Athena's temple, I stand at attention under the blue sky of Africa that seems to scorch everything, I stand at attention as the world takes on the smell of dirt, a distant smell of gods who have not entirely left, and the dirt falls on my face and enters my clenched lips and everyone is looking at Carlos and me and we're the only actors on the world's stage. I feel the dirt of Angola on my lips, I feel it like the taste of the old Achaean coin someone deposited in my mouth to pay for the trip to Hades.

"Punch him, Raúl, or are you some kind of girl?"

It's Marcos speaking, a tall, skinny soldier. There's no solidarity in his words, it's part of the game.

"This one doesn't know how to fight," Carlos says. "These Blacks are going to put a rocket up his ass when they get him, they're gonna use him as their bitch, this one's not even Cuban . . ."

"No, I don't want to be Cuban," I whisper.

"What did you say?" Carlos says. "Repeat it, Marilyn Monroe, so I can answer you. Tell me."

I don't say anything. I know what I'm doing here, but I can't say it, I know why I returned.

Carlos looks around.

"He says he doesn't want to be Cuban. He's a quitter. We'll show him how to be Cuban. Ignacio, bring more dirt over."

Ignacio, the small one—a little soldier who's as slight as myself but who knows martial arts so everyone respects him—fills the infantry shovel with yellow dirt.

"Throw it over the head of this son-of-a-bitch counterrevolutionary worm who doesn't want to be Cuban."

"No, that's not my job," Ignacio says.

"It's an order," Carlos says, and then he says it's a game, and I have to pretend to be a real man, because when we have to fight against the South Africans my mamá won't be there to wipe my ass.

"What's going on here?" says a voice I know well. "Attention, soldiers."

It's the captain, accompanied by Martínez the political officer and the company commanders, Lieutenants Gilberto, Ernesto, Amado, Sergio, and Raymundo. They came up without our noticing. The officers are wearing new camouflage uniforms that stand out against the faded olive green of our own clothing, they're standing in front of us as we suddenly come to attention, avoiding looking directly into their austere, mustached faces.

"Sergeant Carlos Valdivia, explain to me what is happening here," the captain shouts, his voice strident. He looks at the trio made up by Ignacio, who still holds the infantry shovel, although he let the dirt slide out when he stood to attention, Carlos, who hasn't managed to clean his hands, and me, with my face full of yellow dirt, matted by sweat.

"At your command, *compañero capitán*," Carlos shouts, as he was taught at sergeants' school. "I inform you that recruit Raúl Iriarte and I were carrying out a camouflage practice to make the most of our rest time."

"How conscientious of you," Martínez says in a measured voice that hints at mockery. "Now here's a soldier whose sense of honor in combat really goes above and beyond. I congratulate you, Sergeant Carlos Valdivia."

The commander of my company, Lieutenant Amado Salvaterra, nods his head, and the captain comes over, and it's the first time he's looked me right in the eye.

"What's your name, soldier?"

I stand up straight on the Angolan plains. There is no one around me, just a vulture waiting for me to die so it can devour my insides, I'm Prometheus and I'm condemned, at the same time, I am Cassandra and I know I am condemned. I'm standing up straight on the Angolan plains, looking the captain in the eye for the first time, looking into those very dark eyes of a captain from the eastern part of the island with my own blue eyes of a lice-ridden boy they call Marilyn Monroe. The dirt of Angola fills my mouth and is like a premonition, but I don't dare spit it out before I say with a sandy voice, "At your command, Captain. Soldier Raúl Iriarte."

What are you doing here? the captain's eyes seem to be asking. *What are you doing in a Cuban army combat unit in the middle of nowhere?* The captain's eyes seemed to be asking, *What are you doing? Tell me.*

"Soldier Raúl Iriarte, is what Sergeant Carlos Valdivia says the truth?"

"Yes, *compañero capitán.*"

"Are you doubting my word, *compañero capitán?*" Carlos asks.

"This doesn't look like instruction or anything of the sort. It looks like abuse, and this is my unit. You do what I say here, and in my unit, I do not tolerate lowering any soldier's morale. Lieutenant Salvaterra, give the three of them a punishment detail."

"Including the sergeant?"

"The three of them."

A punishment detail. Running with a rucksack full of rocks under the torrid Angolan sun. Ducking down with that rucksack full of rocks, opening a hole in the yellow dirt using an infantry shovel and then filling it in, digging it again, and refilling it ten times. Next to me are Ignacio and Carlos, who whispers to me: "This is your fault, fag, but you'll see, you'll see."

"Leave him alone, Carlos," Ignacio says.

"Stay out of it. I don't care if you're a karate master."

I feel the world receding from me until it's nothing more than a small candle with a flame that barely flickers on the horizon. An Angolan beetle I found is with me alongside the hole I've dug with my shovel, trying to scale a lump of yellow dirt. I look at its translucent black back and feel the world getting further and further away . . . I'm Cassandra, I'm in Ilios and I'm Cassandra, I see that tall, wide-backed shepherd arrive, smiling at the women of Ilios with abundant apathy, and I know that we will lose the whole city because of him, I know he is Paris, I know he is my father's son. I run to the goddess's temple, I fall down before the statue who looks down at me with her painted owl eyes, I feel my mouth filling with saliva, I begin to tremble. Athena speaks through me when she says the city will be lost.

"The city will be lost because of the man who just arrived, who should have died long ago," I say and everyone stares at me.

"What is this madman talking about?" I hear Carlos say before I pass out.

They take me to the infirmary.

It's my birthday and the Russian woman gives me a book by Kierkegaard, the only one I will ever have in my life. It's in English, so I learn English in order to read it. I immerse myself in Kierkegaard when I get back from school. I delve into his ideas like someone returning to the safe harbor he knows. I feel a bit like Abraham, whom that rascally god of the Christians told to kill his son Isaac and then took it back. I read Kierkegaard as it rains, and when it clears, I keep reading Kierkegaard. Athena never has any regrets. If she sends you out to kill someone, it's because she has really thought it through, not to test you. The gods don't need to test you. I was born with my eyes wide open, at least that's what my mother says.

"Your eyes were a light blue that got darker later, Raulito," she says, and takes advantage of my father not being around to dress me up as a girl and pretend that I am her dearly departed sister.

"Little sister, you are prettier every day. I'm going to miss you when I move to Cienfuegos with José, but you'll come with me, right?" she says.

"I don't want to hold you back, Mariela."

"I would never leave you, my little sister, you are the most important thing to me. What are you going to do in filthy Cruces? Come with us, José will agree, he's a bit crude, but he has a heart of gold," Mamá says and smiles at me, caressing my hair, and tells me that if she has a child, perhaps he will be blond-haired and blue-eyed like me, her only sister.

My mother smells like *Tú*-brand eau de toilette. She can play at this all afternoon, she can sit me on her knee and sing me a song and say, "Nancy, tell me about your first boyfriend, that Rolando, tell me about him, he had dark eyes and a twisted mouth because he was a liar, right? And he wanted to take you to Havana, didn't he?"

I have to tell her about a man who is tall and robust, Black as coal, whom I've never seen in my life, and say that he plays the saxophone like no one else and that his smile is like fire, he's a man full of passion.

"So why did you break up?" my mother asks.

"Because he was a real womanizer and one day I caught him in bed with one of the other ballerinas."

"Ah, Mamá was right in not wanting you to go to Havana to study dance, you came back with a swollen belly, then you lost it, and Papá went gray overnight with shame, he who was the best-looking and most honorable man who has ever walked the streets of Cuba."

"He aged because he buried himself in Cruces, because he wanted to, he could have moved to Havana," I replied, so that my mother would go get the dolls and pretend that she and her twin sister were very little and my mother wasn't the studious one, the one who was going to go so far and then didn't go anywhere, and Nancy wasn't the crazy one in the family, the black sheep despite her blond locks. I'm fifteen years old, I am only five feet tall and weigh barely a hundred pounds. My father is just shy of an inch taller than me and about half an inch taller than my brother José, and he thinks that makes him the king of the universe, or he did think so, because he tried to beat on José like he used to, when he would leave him reeling from a rain of blows, and this time José, who spends his time on the roof lifting weights with his friends and doing karate, this time José was the one who hit him, that's why José had to leave home and go live with Flor, his girlfriend with a nursing degree, three years older than him, since my father told him that if he stayed, things would end badly.

"I'm going to teach you a lesson," my father said very seriously, wiping the blood from his face.

My father is also on the verge of going to live with "that fucking Svetlana," as my mother calls the Russian woman, but still, José won't return. He has come to love the streets, he's nineteen years old already and he likes rock and roll and Black women, and my mamá says it's a step backward, that one day he's going to show up with a Black kid and she's not about to brush any nappy hair. My mother brushes my hair, she places a blue bow in it and calls me Nancy. I want to go to my room and keep reading Kierkegaard, I go just like that, dressed like a woman.

turn seventeen and I get the notice from the Military Committee.

"They're not going to take you," my father says in the Russian woman's living room with a glass of vodka in his hands, while Lyudmila, sitting in the other chair, looks at me with that pitying smile that I can't stand. The Russian woman looks much younger than my father and next to him, she's like a movie star, while my father looks filthy and worn-out. Reading has never interested him, but since he started living with the Russian woman, he's become a Raymond Chandler fan. In the Russian woman's living room, there's a large bookcase. The majority of the works are in English since the Russian woman is an English professor at the Institute of Higher Pedagogy in Cienfuegos. I don't know what the Russian woman sees in my father.

When the gray-haired lieutenant colonel, who first checks my genitals and then points for me to sit naked in the same chair where others have sat, asks me if I'm homosexual, I say no. It comes out decisively and the lieutenant colonel, fat and proud, nods in satisfaction.

"Very good," he says. "Raúl Iriarte, you're a little small and scrawny, but we'll make you into a soldier for the socialist fatherland."

I wrote my first poem on an afternoon on which the rain beat down as heavily as my dark thoughts. My first poem was my first portent. I had just read *The Iliad* when, suddenly, the air in my room turned weak and spasmodic, the walls of my room moved away from each other and I could see the pillars etched in stone, and where the low, flat, unadorned ceiling of a socialist-style building had once been, I made out a sky as blue as Cuba's. Before me stood a young man with an intense gaze, bronzed and nude save for a piece of cloth covering his genitals. He was looking at me with intense malevolence, and without him telling me so, I knew he was Apollo.

"This is not my true guise," the god said. "If I revealed to you as I am, you would fall down dead on the spot."

"I know."

"Do you know who you are?"

"I'm Cassandra," I replied. "Or rather, I was Cassandra, and now I am just Raúl Iriarte."

"You don't stop being who you are just because you have died," Apollo replied, and I knew I was going to write a poem, unprompted, that I was an oracle.

"You will return to the Old World to die again, and that is your sentence, to repeat the cycle for eternity, you are Achilles, but you are also the turtle."

I don't know if the god said this last part or if I dreamt it, because I felt myself falling into the void. I began to shake and when I woke up, the lines of the checkerboard floor of my house had lined up again and I saw the Achaean vessels heading to Ilios, I saw them, a snakelike line of boats smaller than the one my father used to take us to the bay of Cienfuegos. I discerned the sails and I discerned the oars submerging themselves in the Hellespont, I woke up with a startle and wanted to warn Hecuba, but it was too late, the downpour was taking me to Cuba, it was turning my reality into that of Raúl Iriarte, the Spineless. I went back to being Spineless and my Cuban mother was looking at me.

"You have a fever," she said. "You don't have to go to school."

I sat down on the bed when my mother left the room, opened my notebook for math, the subject I hated most, and on the last page, I wrote a poem that spoke of spring in Ilios when evening falls and you go to the shores of the beach in search of shipwrecks and shells.

I was in seventh grade, my aunt Nancy had died, and I didn't want to stay with my mother and her very sad ways, I didn't want to be there when she would sigh and say it was better to be dead. So I got dressed despite the fever, I took the bus and went to school. In the afternoon, I had literary workshop. A recent literature grad with a sullen and tired air about him, sent to our school by the Provincial Library of Cienfuegos, would sit before the six students who had chosen literature over chess and other sports, and would read us poems by César Vallejo, Nicolás Guillén, Roberto Fernández Retamar, Roque Dalton, and Mario Benedetti, who was his favorite, he liked him so much that he had memorized many of his poems. He would rise up in his chair and begin to recite them, gesticulating wildly with his hands in an exaggerated way. Then we would analyze our own work, which generally dealt with how good our parents were and how sad we would be without them, and with our socialist fatherland, and, every once in a while, with love.

The first one to read was Katia, a girl from my class who sat three desks ahead of me and with whom I got along rather well. Then Rogelio Camejo, whom I remember as a redhead with countless freckles, which had earned him the nickname the Freckle. We listened to their poems without offering any opinion, just nodding our heads, and then we all clapped, including the teacher, who said they were very good. Then it was my turn, I stood up and began to read, and as I went on, I saw how the teacher's face, already long, stretched out even longer. When I finished, he said, "That poem isn't realistic, it's metaphysical and decadent. It reminds me of Cavafy. Where did you copy it from?"

"Nowhere," I said, and the teacher ended the workshop.

My classmates went out in one group. I remained in my seat and he put away his glasses in their case with a tired gesture and stood up.

"Let's go see the principal," he said.

I go to the head office with the teacher to argue with the principal, Eugenio Enrique Álvarez de la Nuez, about my obvious ideological weaknesses. It's 3:40 in the afternoon and the principal, relaxed behind his desk, listening to a classical music station on the radio, asks the literature specialist and me to sit down in the two wooden chairs.

"What's the problem?" he asks, turning off the device. "Don't tell me he got into a fight, because Raulito is very calm."

"Worse—he showed up with a very inappropriate poem. It was quite frightening, and believe me, I'm not the kind who is easily scared by just anything. So I wanted to make sure you knew."

"Something erotic? Naughty?"

"Worse."

"Really? Let's see, Raúl Iriarte, read that poem, right now . . ."

My hands are shaking so much that I think I can't concentrate. But I finally manage to read.

"Where did you copy it from?" the principal asks when I finish reading. He's not as alarmed as the Benedetti admirer. "Surely you were rummaging around in old books. But be careful with what you copy, Raulín. I have enough problems at this school without falling into ideological diversionism. Bring your parents in tomorrow. Thank you, *profesor*."

He gets up from his chair and holds out his hand to the teacher, a clear sign that the meeting is over.

"I don't want you in the workshop anymore. It's not because of you, it's because I don't want any problems, they tell you there's no issue but then they start studying you, and, you know, a chain is only as strong as its weakest link. Good luck, Raúl Iriarte—you're going to need it if you keep writing like that," the teacher whispered when we were outside the office. He gave me a quick hug and I was left to watch his hasty retreat, until he was out of sight.

Before going home, I ripped up the piece of paper on which I had written the poem and threw it in the trash.

I had a fever.

Y ou have a fever," my mother said that spring day in 1980, just before they broadcast the images from the Peruvian embassy on the TV.

The Peruvian embassy had begun to get famous, ever since thousands of people from Havana had taken refuge there as they waited for an exit permit, and I'm sitting with José, who came to visit us with Irma, his stunning, tall, dark-skinned girlfriend, who, she claimed, was kicked out of the Cuban National Ballet for being Black. She says that Alicia Alonso ran her hand over her head and said, when she felt her hair, "Go back to Cienfuegos."

"Alicia Alonso is blind?" I asked.

"As a mole," said the former ballerina.

"She was right," my mother says from the kitchen. "Who's ever seen a Black Giselle? Alicia put too much work into making that ballet what it is for someone to ruin it for her now."

My brother doesn't say anything, and neither does his girlfriend. My brother looks at me with intense hatred, as if he believes that I agree with the words flying at us from the kitchen, worn words, old as the almond leaves that linger on in the park. My brother's girlfriend's eyes are liquid, a golden shade that I'll recall when I see the humps of gazelles in Africa, but right now, they just seem sad.

"Is this what you brought me here for?" José's girlfriend whispers as she squeezes his hand.

"Shut up, Ma," my brother says. "Stop talking shit."

"I'm not talking shit, you mind how you talk to me," my mother says, still from the kitchen. "So now I can't even speak in my own home?"

My mother also wanted to be a ballerina, but she married while she was very young. In the living room, there's a photo that testifies to the moment: my father in a *dril cien* linen suit that looks somewhat big on him and my mother wearing a flower-print dress. They both smile at the camera. Behind the car they rented to go to Havana, a blue-and-silver Buick, rises the silhouette of the capitol building. Their honeymoon was at the Ambos Mundos hotel, the same one where Hemingway stayed, and my father would say that he saw him going out in shorts and a Hawaiian-print shirt with a daiquiri in hand, although the writer was dead by then. My father didn't know about his suicide. He has always been ignorant, a liar, and a charlatan. In this photo, he looks happy. Not my mother, my mother has an air about her of separateness, obstinacy, and melancholy, as if it were raining inside of her, not a downpour but a soft rain, a snow shower that her Asturias-born grandmother brought with her. But anyway, that afternoon we were sitting together, my brother, his girlfriend, and I, watching the old Soviet TV set, seeing the people of Havana pour like an overflowing river into the embassy of that country that sounds familiar from elementary school classes about the Incas and El Dorado and that is no longer a mystical, magical place, but a concrete destination to which thousands of Cubans now aim to go. My brother and his girlfriend watch TV holding hands, without saying anything, quieter than the evening that falls quietly, but I know that soon it will be in both of their heads. Let's leave, my brother will think, let's leave, the girlfriend will think, I know it, and they'll leave. They'll take a speedboat that will leave them in Kanye West, really far from Peru, but first they'll get eggs thrown at them, and there will be a rock among the eggs, and my brother's girlfriend will lose an eye, so they'll part ways and it'll be *adiós, negrita,* don't let the door hit you on the way out. I'm seventeen years old, I finished high school with excellent grades, I'll be entering the army in no time, and if I make an effort, I can get into the university, but Apollo told me, "No university for you, none of that. Why delay your return to the infinite? The blazing wheel of transmutations awaits you."

'll arrive in Angola like an invisible bird for the captain, I'll be just one more among the thousands of little Cuban soldiers, more or less hairy, all trying to leave their baby faces behind. The heavy green rucksack will be my wings. I'll hear him harangue the troops, utter his "homeland or death," while I'm just one new element of the first squad of the second company, an infantryman among other infantrymen, and only when Carlos pours the Angolan dirt over me will the captain see me differently, and order Lieutenant Amado, following the punishment detail, to take me to his office, he'll tell him without any further explanation, he won't look into his eyes when he commands him, he will simply kick up a little bit of dust with his left boot, shod in an almost-new Romanian boot, and say: "Send me that little blond soldier, I need to speak with him."

He's waiting for me inside the tent, seated behind a folding desk, in a folding chair, he smells like *Tú* eau de toilette, the same one my mother uses, and he is freshly shaven. I stand before him, I lift my hand up in a military salute and say, "At your command." He orders me at ease and looks into my eyes. I know what he is going to say, in a whisper that reaches me long before the words come out of his mouth.

"You are from Cienfuegos, right? I've been to that city. It's very pretty. I was there for a July 26th celebration, and I loved it. In any event, you can't let them abuse you—it doesn't look good. That Carlos is a deviant, but he's a good sergeant. The other soldiers listen to him, so I can't demote him, but I will tell him that if he goes on like this, I'll have to see what I can do with him."

His voice sounds deep, full of dry and disagreeable intonations, it's a masculine voice. I am standing before him, although he already said "At ease," then he comes close to me and pats my head, just that, with a gesture that aims to be paternal but that I recognize all too well, because it's the same as the one my teacher gave me, the one who spoke to me of forbidden books, back in tenth grade. He is my nemesis, although he doesn't know it.

"Do you have good handwriting?" he asks later, and it's as if he is asking why my eyes are such a deep blue.

"Yes," I reply, because Apollo, standing before me, has transmitted the response, "and I'm a good writer too."

"Really? Sit down and write something, whatever you want. It can be a letter to my wife, who's blond like you. I need a secretary. I can't take care of everything, and I'm sick of that Martínez. All he thinks about is playing baseball, even though his degree is in journalism—the only kind of reporting that interests him is sports journalism."

I sit down in the chair where he was sitting until now, he places a notebook and pen in front of me and I wait for him to dictate something, but he doesn't, so I start to write. He comes close and I feel his body heat and the breathing of a thickset man.

Outside, a bird sings, a young leopard preys on the villagers' cattle about twenty miles away, and the town's prominent elders, led by a robust man with a very white beard and a rustic staff, come to the unit with their fearful eyes locked on their bare feet, dirtied by the red earth.

"*Precisamos matar a fera mosqueada*," the old man will say in a Portuguese so clear that the captain will require no translation.

"We didn't come here to kill leopards," the captain will reply, but then, when he sees the villagers' tear-filled eyes and their shaking hands, he will nod his head three times. "Why don't you kill it?" he will ask.

"We don't have the means, the soldiers took all of our weapons," one of the other old men, notable for his robust neck ringed by metal chains and wild seeds, will reply in Portuguese.

"So we'll go and kill it, then," the captain will say a few minutes later. "Martínez, are you in?"

"Yes, Captain, that's the kind of mess I like to sort out."

"Go get three more soldiers, the best shots in the battalion," the captain will say, and will look to me so that I can be proud of him. This has yet to happen. I see the leopard's silhouette gliding very close to the straw huts, I see those eyes that seem tame in the evening light, and I know it will die, and I am pained by the death of the young leopard, its corpse left to the mercy of hyenas and vultures.

My beloved, it has been very hot today, almost as hot as an August day in Cuba. I sat with my subordinates to watch the sunrise and I thought of you and realized how much I miss you. You are the only woman for me, the most beautiful.

I write, thinking of Mariela, my mother in this life, I see her rocking in her chair and singing one of those songs she likes so much, something by Silvio Rodríguez, alone, because after my father left, Mariela was never with anyone else again. Something inside her died when my father left. I see her before me, as the shape of my handwriting appears like discrete curves on the letter I'm writing for the captain. I hear him panting behind me, touching me without touching me, his hands resting on the back of my chair, very close to my neck.

"You're so small, so fragile, how did they let you in?" he says. "You look like a young girl . . . Read me what you've written so far, please."

That "please" hides something intimate, it goes beyond what an officer says to a mere tin soldier like me. I go to stand, but he asks me to remain seated, he remains standing behind me, I cannot see him, my voice comes out dry and virile but with a soft and agitated edge, I think about the leopard between the trees, waiting for night to fall so it can prey on the peasants' cattle, I think of its calmly cruel eyes. I raise my voice to read the letter, it's like when I was still in elementary school and the teacher would point at me with her ringed hand: "Let's see—you read, Raulito." I'm very careful with the pauses at each comma, I stop for a second at each period and enunciate each letter. When I'm done, the captain asks me to stand up and he hugs me. His eyes have teared up.

"Thank you, soldier, you can go back to your quarters."

My quarters are an enormous tent that I share with six other recruits and a private first class. The private first class is named Matías Benítez but everyone calls him Santiago because he is from that city. The soldiers are Fermín Portela, or Johnny the Rocker; Amaury Valdez, also known as the Gangster because he wants only what doesn't belong to him; Juan Izquierdo, or Pretty Boy, because of his strut; Manuel Cifuentes, whom we call simply Manuel; Agustín, my friend from Cienfuegos, whom some call Muscle Man, for obvious reasons; and me, Marilyn Monroe. In the closest tent, to the right, the six sergeants sleep. There sleeps Carlos, who, one night when the company commander is off duty in Luanda, comes into our lodging and yells "Attention" so that we all stand and then forces us to do our daily calisthenics at three in the morning. We go out into the cold of the African night and outside, Martínez, the political officer, is waiting for us. He and Carlos were drinking Angolan aguardiente, it's clear. Martínez, Miramar's boy wonder, and Carlos, the outcast of Matanzas, have a taste for abuse in common. We start with squats, and when our legs can't take it anymore, we go to push-ups.

"This is for your own good," Martínez says, "you have to be strong and prepared for any mission that the homeland requires. The mandrills are very dangerous."

The mandrills are the Angolans.

When Martínez is drunk, racism rises like the tide to the shores of his mouth. Carlos, who is darker-skinned than some Angolans, laughs and then comes close, with a gun in hand, and puts his right foot on my ass. I'm trying to do a push-up with that heavy boot, with Carlos's heavy foot, on my ass.

"Get up, whore, be a man!"

I can't take it anymore and remain lying down on the ground, I drag myself like a sorry snake and then turn over. Carlos puts the gun to my temple.

"Do the push-ups, whore!"

"Leave him alone already," I hear Martínez's voice behind me. "That's all for now, you can return to your hammocks."

Martínez throws an arm around Carlos's back.

"You're drunk . . ." he says with an inebriated laugh. "You all have to learn to be men. This is for your own good."

Carlos lowers his weapon and frees himself from the officer's grip. He keeps looking at me for a while and then says, "If anyone goes and tattles to the captain they'll have to deal with me."

"Don't worry about that. I'm an officer of the Revolutionary Armed Forces, and I will be respected," Martínez says. Then he straightens out his uniform and turns toward Carlos.

"Sergeant, take the men to their lodging."

"Squad, attention!" Carlos yells as loud as his lungs allow.

We stand before their two dark silhouettes in the Angolan night.

"Return to your hammocks, go on, quickly, we mean now!"

We run to our hammocks. It's four in the morning and it's cold here in Cunene.

That night, Agustín, lying to my right, says to me, "When we go into action, I'm going to kill him. They'll think it was a South African."

He doesn't have to tell me who, I know he means Carlos, but I don't say anything. Agustín will not kill Carlos and both will return to Cuba, decorated veterans. They will both study afterward at the same wide-doored university. I will not return to Cuba, I'm going to die here, at the margins of the Old World.

N o, there must be a mistake here, they've really done it this time," my father said when I told him they had declared me suitable to join the Revolutionary Armed Forces. "I'm going over there right now to sort all this shit out."

I see him, thin, haggard, with week-old stubble and muscly arms. He looks like one of those scrawny assassins who turn up at the bar where Nick Adams works in Hemingway's "The Killers," which I had just read in an anthology that was published in Cuba, *The Snows of Kilimanjaro*. My father takes the shirt he always leaves forgotten on the back of the chair and stands up. The Russian woman, much taller than he is and with a delicate and somewhat dazed face, also stands up. I remember her like that, with her flower-print dress of synthetic cotton, under which I could make out her underwear. My father hits her, not very hard or very often, just every once in a while, when he gets jealous of the Russian woman's friendship with a physics professor at the pedagogical institute, a robust Black man, and he shakes her strongly by the shoulders.

"Calm down, José Raúl," the Russian woman says now, looking my father in the eye. "You're not going to solve anything by yelling. I'm sure everything can be cleared up if you're decent and polite."

"They're going to have to listen to me. Look at this miserable boy, how short and small he is, do you think he's made for the army? This son of a bitch is going to school."

He puts on his shirt and we go out. The Chevy has been at the mechanic's for almost a month, so we walk to the bus stop. It's cold, the morning is lovely, and the Russian woman and I are in spontaneously high spirits, as if something good were about to happen. Not my father. My father is very serious, he's worried about me. My father loves me, it's rare for me to have proof of it. The Russian woman and I talk about poetry, he doesn't understand a word, then we talk about *War and Peace* while we wait for the bus, and although he hasn't read it, he feels obliged to offer an opinion, he says the Russians are boring, monotonous.

"I meant the writers," he clarifies, because Lyudmila is shooting him a serious look, "and please, be quiet, I can't think straight.

"I can't think straight," my father says on that November morning, when I am about to hand over my bones to the care of the Revolutionary Armed Forces. "I can't think straight," he says and drags the Russian woman and me to a delusional meeting with the head of Cienfuegos's Military Committee so he can investigate my case. He takes a good look at my scant stature, at my thin body, at my sticklike arms.

"What can you get out of a recruit like that?" my father asks Colonel Gerardo Iglesias Morales, when he's finally agreed to a meeting with us after a two-hour wait.

The colonel scratches his shaved head and looks, not into

my father's eyes, but first at the Russian woman's tits, and then at me.

"It's true that he's very short, but so was Napoleon Bonaparte, and look how far he got. Men are not measured from the ground to their heads, but rather from their heads to the heavens."

"But he's no Napoleon," my father says. "He spends his days shut up in his room, reading, he barely goes out, I assure you . . . and he's a little mad."

"Where is the medical certificate verifying his madness? You didn't bring it? You don't have it? Then there's nothing more to discuss, it seems to me, *compañero* José Raúl Iriarte. You're trying to get your son out of the duty of every young Cuban. I assure you that in the army, he will become a man."

"He's already a man," my father says, looking at me with an expression I didn't understand then, but now that I'm in the Elysian Fields, taking pleasure in the couplets of the same sirens who bewitched Odysseus, I understand it all too well. My father looks at me sadly, that man whom I looked down on, whom I considered only good for spending hours beneath a truck or a car, or on top of the Russian woman, bringing her to orgasms that made her forget that she wanted to pass as a Cuban woman, that made her speak in the language of Tolstoy—that man was capable of feeling pain, of predicting that he would lose his son.

"He will come back from Angola and we'll be fine," the Russian woman says when we're riding back on the bus.

"Let's hope so."

We part ways at the corner and I return to the house of my mother, who still doesn't know that when I turn eighteen, I'm leaving for Angola.

"What are you looking for over there?" she'll say when she finds out. "My child, you know that almost all of us came from Asturias, and that my Black great-grandfather, who gave me this cinnamon-colored skin that so fascinated your father before he became the son of a bitch that he is now, he wasn't any part Angolan, he was a Black man who came from Louisiana, who spoke Spanish with a slight French accent, he was a very refined gentleman, yessir, not just any old Black man. Tell them you're not going, do your service here, any place is good enough to be of service to the homeland. Will you do it, my child? Will you?"

I don't say anything, it's raining softly, just barely, I go toward the balcony and take a look outside. I don't want to lie to my mother. The gods are watching and judging me, I'm going to go and I won't return. I see Angola before I arrive, I see Angola and the feline with the spotted back who proudly lifts his head, awaiting me. The gods of the Old World await me, the dog-headed Anubis awaits me, Isis and Osiris and the souls of all kings past await me, and the old African gods await me, the ones who crossed the sea and now return with me, Athena awaits me as well as Apollo, their essences already taking the forms of gods.

The second time the captain ordered me to go to his tent, it was so that I could write, with the best penmanship possible, another letter to his wife, whom he described as a being of light, an angel who studied industrial engineering, who tumbled south from Havana to Gibara and into love with him.

"Katerina Rodríguez Morales, that's her name. She has blue eyes like you. Write down that I love her very much and that I'll be back, and sit here."

He pointed at another folding chair, very close to his own, and he watched me write. It was about four in the afternoon. The shouts of other soldiers playing baseball reached us from outside. The captain was very close to me and smelled like *Tú* eau de toilette, like my mother. If he leaned over just a bit, our faces would touch.

"You don't have to shave, it's true. You're so lucky to be so smooth-faced—I wear out a blade every day. I'm very hairy," he said, smiling.

I contemplated his rough, eastern peasant's face, very Spanish with a hint of Black, and I didn't say anything.

"You don't talk much. You're always so quiet . . . You seem like a shy girl."

I was about to tell him that my mamá used to dress me as a girl and pretend I was Nancy, her sister who died of cancer.

"That's right, focus on the letter, it has to be perfect," he said, and then: "What a complexion!" he said, and stroked my face with his hand.

"You're practically a girl, it's incredible that you're eighteen years old. How old would you say I am?"

"Twenty-five," I said, although he looked about eight thousand years old to me.

"You're being easy on me, come on, make a guess."

"Forty."

"Now you've gone too far. I'm thirty-five . . . Do I seem very old to you?"

He placed his hand on my right knee when he asked that and looked into my eyes.

He looked into my eyes.

There was a dry, intense heat, from outside came the shouts of the other soldiers, Agustín was lying down in the infirmary with a fever, the leopard stretched out, ready to prey on the villagers' cattle, and the African sun was setting on the horizon. He placed that bronzed hand on my olive-green uniform pants and everything began to happen. I didn't feel anything, I've never felt anything. I don't know what sexual desire is. I am Cassandra and I'm just passing through, I wanted to say that, but I didn't. I knew it. I knew that the captain would suddenly lean over me and that he was going to kiss me on the lips, a light, slight kiss, hardly a kiss at all, but that would create a secret between us, a complicity beyond us. I knew that Lieutenant Martínez was about to enter the tent, "With your permission, Captain," and that he would put some distance between us and say, "Keep writing, soldier Raúl Iriarte, and do me a favor and watch your spelling," and I also knew that the young UNITA guerrilla had already received his directive to attack the Cuban camp. I knew that Martínez, looking at the captain and at me, without suspecting anything, was already a dead man, although he would smile widely enough to then say, "Wanna play ball with us, Captain?"

"Can't you see I'm busy here?" the captain said without standing up, giving Martínez a dark, intense look.

"Ah, but that can wait," Martínez said. "We need a fourth hitter and you're the best. Don't make me plead! Let this little soldier wrap up here, come on—you're the leader, and it's good to encourage a sense of teamwork among the troops."

Martínez didn't look at me for a second, I still remember him, naked from the waist up, his camouflage plants sullied by red dirt, tall and ruddy, with a smile that extended from his mouth all the way up to his steel-gray eyes.

"Okay, I'm coming," the captain said. "Let me change and I'll come right out. Tell them to wait for me."

"That's the spirit!" Martínez cheered, and went outside.

We were left alone. The captain stood up and looked at me, calculating whether he should crush me with one of his Romanian boots. Then he put a hand on my back and said, "If you tell anyone what happened between us, I'll kill you, and it can never happen again. Is that clear?"

"Yes, *compañero capitán*," I said, standing up and issuing a military salute.

"Why do you have to be so pretty? You're like a girl. If you left your hair long, you'd be beautiful . . . They call you Marilyn Monroe, right?"

"Yes."

"And what do you say to them? You let them?"

"They outnumber me."

"Who are 'they'? Tell me and I'll take steps right away. Is Carlos one of them? Tell me."

You know he is, Captain, I could have said, *you hear everything from your tent, when we go out to the leisure area on weekends and the soldiers get bored and then there I am, the weakest one, to entertain them, you know that.* But I didn't say anything, I remained stiff and he took two steps back, as if he needed to observe me from a certain distance.

"Don't let anyone push you around. If they keep doing it, you come and tell me, is that clear?"

"I'm not a rat."

"It's not being a rat. It's fulfilling the duties of a revolutionary, and our duty is to keep up our fighting spirit. Do you understand?"

"Yes, I understand."

"Read me the letter."

"I'm not done yet."

"Okay, read me what you have so far."

Sí, compañero capitán. Sí, compañero capitán. Sí, compañero capitán. Sí, compañero capitán. Sí, compañero capitán. Sí, compañero capitán. Sí, compañero capitán. Sí, compañero capitán. Sí, compañero capitán. Sí, compañero capitán. Sí, compañero capitán. Sí, compañero capitán. Sí, compañero capitán. Sí, compañero capitán. My job is to repeat "Sí, compañero capitán." Sí, compañero capitán. Sí, compañero capitán. Sí, compañero capitán. Sí, compañero capitán. Sí, compañero capitán. Sí, compañero capitán. Sí, compañero capitán. Sí, compañero capitán. Sí, compañero capitán. Sí, compañero capitán. Sí, compañero capitán. Sí, compañero capitán. Sí, compañero capitán. Sí, compañero capitán. Sí, compañero capitán. Sí, compañero capitán.

I go out dressed as a woman. It is the Feast of the Holy Innocents and my mother has given me permission to go to a costume party. She gives me permission to take revenge on my father, who ran off with the Russian woman. She did my hair herself, did my makeup, and then loaned me a beautiful light blue dress that once belonged to Nancy. The costume party is at my school. The Spanish and literature teacher put it together. That teacher who once spoke to me of Virgilio Piñera and Lezama and of a writer who had recently left Cuba for Miami, one Reinaldo Arenas, who had been his friend back in Havana and who wrote a book called *Singing from the Well*, about a mad boy. He told me all of this before putting his hand on my thigh and looking into my eyes and confessing he went "the other way."

"This is the first time I've told anyone, and it's very dangerous. If you tell anyone else, Rauli, you could get me into a lot of trouble. I could get thrown out of the party and of school."

"So why are you telling me?" I asked, and he put his right hand on my thigh.

"Because it was eating me up. You don't know what it's like

to live this way, pretending to be something else . . . I trust you, Rauli, you're very special. I like you. You're going to be a writer."

"I don't think so. I'm going to die very young."

"Oh, don't be silly, forget it. Look, take this book, but then bring it back to me. I hope no one sees you with it."

We're in the Spanish and literature office and the teacher stands up and takes down a book covered with the front page of *Bohemia* magazine from one of the bookcases. "*Paradiso*," the initial pages say.

"Put it away and take very good care of it for me. It's a gift from Lezama himself," the teacher says. "Don't let your father see it. He already has it in for me."

I have to cross the city dressed as a woman. Athena and Apollo go with me. One on each side, disguised as the orishas Obatalá and Shango, they accompany me so that nothing happens to me, because today is not my day to die. I'm a girl walking through the city called Cienfuegos, and the passersby stop to look at me.

"What a pretty blonde," someone whispers as I go by.

My mother sent me to meet my death. My mother sacrificed me to take revenge on my father, her eyes were tearing up when she kissed me on the cheek, taking care not to ruin my makeup. I am fifteen years old and I walk through the city dressed like a woman. Dressed as a woman, I wait for the bus, and if I'm asked my name, I will say Cassandra, but no one asks me anything, I'm just one more girl in a city by the sea, who's almost the sea herself, who waits for the bus. When I get on, a young man stands up and offers me his seat.

I'm going to get to the school and recite a Darío poem.

Margarita, está linda la mar
y el viento
lleva esencia sutil de azahar:
tu aliento.

I'm going to recite it before my classmates who are dressed as independence fighters, Superman, or werewolves, before girls dressed as Little Red Riding Hood, Sleeping Beauty, the Kolkhoz Woman, Vietnamese or Angolan girls. None is more feminine than me, none prettier than me.

"This one's queerer than a three-dollar bill," one of my classmates says loudly.

"If he's not a fairy, he knows where they keep the pixie dust," another one says.

But the prize for the best costume will be for me, for Cassandra. I will take it to my mother, a chocolate cake that we will eat together, seasoned with tears shed by my mother, who is crying because she thinks everything in her life is over, my naïve mother who doesn't know the worst is to come, that she will face the death of her sons, navigate that, leave that on the deck of the vessel of her life and continue on. She has yet to say to herself, *Look at this starry night without her by my side.* Her is me, Cassandra.

One day I told her, "José and I are going to die."

She didn't want to understand.

It was on one of those days that my brother once again went looking for something to steal so he could sell it and buy drugs.

"I need a hit!" José would shout, and I was young, but I already knew what my brother needed a hit of: Parkisonil with ninety-proof alcohol. I knew he would come, so I told my mamá that we should hide the TV set so he wouldn't take it. She didn't listen to me because I'm Cassandra, the one no one believes, and my brother took the old Russian TV set, my brother pushed my mother, he threw her against a wall and called her a whore and yelled "faggot" at me and told me he'd heard about the party at my school and my wearing a woman's dress, and that he was ashamed of us, a faggot and a crazy whore who thought her younger son was Nancy.

"Mariela, it's your fault he's like this," José said, the TV set already in his arms, as he struggled to open the door without dropping the thing.

"Did that Black whore you're running around with push you to steal from your own family? I'm going to the police!" yelled my mother, but she never went.

'm sixteen years old and the sea holds my happiness. I go to the beach, with an Edgar Allan Poe book in hand, and I look into the distance. The Russian woman is sitting next to me; she brought me here so we could talk.

"Listen, Raulito, you're a teenager already. The heart has its own reasons that the mind can never understand. Your father and I . . . Your father and I let, allowed, couldn't avoid things getting to the point of no return, but look—your father loves you very much, even if he may seem very crude at times, he's always thinking of your brother and especially of you, since you're the youngest, you need so much from him, and . . ."

I'm not listening, but I like to be next to the Russian woman, I like feeling that she understands me. I understand her too. The Russian woman is as mad as I am; you'd have to be to fall in love with my father. The Russian woman sees something in my father that I don't, no matter how hard I try, to me, he is just that short guy who scratches himself between the legs without any concern for who's around, but to the Russian woman he is a kind of knight in shining armor, a beautiful man.

ll over less than an inch," my father says two years later
when he goes to see me with my unit, just before my departure for Angola, that last time my parents and I are together.

He says this as he looks me straight in the eye, very serious,
feeling guilty over having given me that extra inch that made me
fit for the army.

"You shouldn't have forced him to drink goat's milk. He
didn't want to, but you insisted," my mother says, and her eyes
are full of intense reproach for issues beyond those at hand.

I look at them. Both have aged overnight, time covers them
with a greenish patina, made up of equal parts disappointment
and fear. They're afraid I won't return, that it will be like with my
brother, who now lives ninety miles away and it's as if he didn't
exist.

"Yesterday, a State Security agent came to see me," my father told my mother one very hot afternoon. "José goes around
talking shit about this revolution that has given him everything.
Forget that you have a son."

"You can forget if you want," my mother replied. "For me,

he will always be my son, and I don't care what that son of a bitch Fidel says."

That son of a bitch Fidel.

I was there when my mother said these words and my father lifted his hand to strike her, but I grabbed a knife and said, "No, Papá."

I grabbed it because when my father raises a hand, you never know how it's going to end. He begins to hit and gets more worked up with each blow, first a slap for Mamá, then a kick in the stomach for me, and then he slams his own head against the wall, the sound of it going *tum-tum* until the neighbors come and ask, "What's going on?"

I'm fifteen years old, my father sees me with the knife at chest level in front of him, he sees the shaking blade of the knife, and then he looks me in the eye. My hair is long, almost to my neck. If I look in the mirror, I seem like a silent film actress, with my hair in a bob, but I am Cassandra and I lift the knife in front of my father and I know what will happen, he'll gather everything, or almost everything, and put it in a suitcase, he'll gather his filthy mechanic's overalls, his guayaberas, his only good jeans, his chess set and his weights, he'll fit them any way he can in the case and he'll go to the Russian woman's house. I see him, a small man with the strength of a chimpanzee, dragging the case down the stairs. My father has left and my mother has struck me very hard.

"This is for threatening your father. Don't do it again. No one should interfere between a husband and wife."

My mother is going to lose the two men in her life, my father, who was, in reality, no longer her man, but rather the Russian woman's, and she will soon lose my brother José, but I don't say anything. I remain silent while I stare her in the eye. I am not my mother's man and we both know it, she thinks I am her sister Nancy and, when she thinks I am asleep, she comes close and caresses my hair and calls me Nancy and sometimes, when she's hit the bottle too hard, she insists that I dress up like a woman.

"Come on, do it for me."

I put on my aunt's skinny-woman dresses, I put on the heels, I make myself up and go out to the living room, and she doesn't call me Nancy because she doesn't dare, it would stimulate my madness and her own, but I can see in her eyes that she thinks I am Nancy. My mother also thinks that I'm homosexual, that I like men, but I don't feel anything. When that literature teacher who spoke to me of forbidden writers kissed me, all I felt was that his mouth smelled a bit like poor-quality cigarettes, and when he took my hand to his erect member, I didn't feel anything then, either, it was like grabbing a cylinder full of meat. I started to move my hand because he asked me to.

go out to watch the captain and the others play baseball. I'd actually rather go back to my quarters, open up a book, and start reading, but I go and sit on the grass next to two other soldiers and I watch the players. There are eighteen of them, nine on each team. Out of all of them, seven won't return to Cuba. They will remain here, fertilizing the African earth. Martínez will return in a box tapered at the end. But today, they look young and vigorous as they shout at the top of their lungs, grip the bat, and run in the grass of this country that never saw baseball before the Cubans arrived.

The captain doesn't even look at me out of the corner of his eye as he plays, it's as if I didn't exist to him. Carlos does look at me and hates me.

"Marilyn Monroe, you fag, you rat, I'm going to kill you," he tells me at one point as he walks by, very close to me.

He doesn't have good enunciation, it's as if his words emerge from his mouth through a complicated process. I don't fear him or hate him, I just look at him and know that he likes me. If I liked him, everything would be easier, I think, but that's not how it is. I don't like the captain, either, naked from the waist up, almost as muscular as Carlos and much more so than Martínez and the other officers. I don't like anyone. I'm sitting next to two other soldiers who are watching the baseball game. The one closest to me is called Alfredo Rojas and he's a very skinny kid who keeps cheering on the captain's team because he's from the eastern part of the island, like him. Martínez's is the Havana team, although he's the only one who's actually from Havana, the rest are from Matanzas, Pinar del Río, and Villa Clara. The best player on that team is Agustín, who's languishing with fever in the infirmary.

"Hit it, kid, hit it!" Alfredo Rojas yells at the top of his lungs.

The other soldier, also to my right, is Johnny the Rocker, they call him that because he loves rock and roll, and he says he wants to go into combat and kill some South Africans and some Blacks.

"I came because I love the idea of fighting, of feeling the AK firing and seeing the guys fall down like rag dolls," he says in one of the political background classes Martínez usually leads.

"No, soldier, you came to settle a debt with humanity, to help other peoples like so many helped ours," Martínez says with a haughty voice, and it's as if he believes in what he is saying.

"Yeah, yeah," Johnny says, "whatever you say. But how long, Lieutenant? We've been in Africa for almost six months already with no action. At least let us go to the *quimbos* and rape the Black women a little."

He was laughing as he said this and everyone else broke out in laughter and Martínez smiled because it's a joke and we were sitting on Angola's yellow dirt and Carlos said those Black women didn't have to be raped, just be given it good and hard, because they were horny as could be thanks to the monkey meat they ate.

"They hunt the chimpanzees and eat them, that's why there are almost none left."

"How do you know anything about that, Carlitín?" Martínez looked shocked, although everyone knew that Carlos, Martínez, and three other soldiers went to the *quimbo*, to the house of a Portuguese *mulata* who ran a brothel. They paid her with cans of condensed milk, went over in their jeep and returned at night. With them went Marcos, a small FAPLA sergeant who served as interpreter and guide. Everyone knew, the captain knew. "Exploring" was how the captain referred to it.

Now I'm watching the ball travel from one glove to another, I see the players, fixed in my memory, I see the leopard lying in wait near the encampment, I see it, beyond the scrub circling the perimeter, but more than the whole leopard, I see its dead, yellow eyes, because the leopard is already dead, we've come all the way to Africa to kill a leopard. Then I feel someone approaching me, practically a giant, who looks at me, and in his dark, golden eyes there is a resentment that goes beyond the life we're currently living, a resentment that reeks of old ships crossing the Hellespont and memories of what was not and will not be, the giant has a wound in his abdomen with rotting edges, but he doesn't see Raúl or Nancy or Wendy or Marilyn Monroe: he sees Cassandra. I see him and I'm in Ilios again, standing at the walls alongside my father and my younger siblings, hugging the youngest, Laodice, who trembles, and her heart beating alongside mine is barely a murmur. I look at my father's face, I look at his wrinkled hands that can no longer raise a spear, I look at the archers who launch their arrows from the walls, I see Paris and his elusive eyes, Paris who avoids looking at me. Then I look down and see Ajax, I see the enormous shield hanging from his shoulders and I see him raise his sword that glints over the head of Teucer, my cousin.

"No!" I yell and my voice gets lost among the humming of the other women and the old men and the snapping of the arrows that Apollo prevents from hitting their targets. I watch Teucer fall, son of no one, my lover, I watch as this man who now looks at me, Ajax son of Telamon, slits his throat and then seeks out another victim. He is now standing before me, unseen by anyone but me, and his eyes are full of rancor. It is as if he were accusing me of something, as if he had forgotten that the one responsible for his death was Odysseus, whom the gods preferred above all mortals.

"Oh, daughter of Priam, the divine Peleus's weapons were for me, not for the perfidious Odysseus," he says.

"It's true, son of Telamon, you are right, but what can I do?"

"Nothing. I wanted you to know, for everyone to know, that Achilles's weapons were for me, not for that dog from Ithaca," the specter says and disappears, sand in the sand, dust in the dust.

"Look out!" someone shouts and the baseball hits me in the head.

I'm at the infirmary. Agustín is sweating out his fever in the other hammock. I look up at the cloth ceiling and hear him whimpering. He's sick, but he'll survive. In three days, the great march will begin, we'll climb into the armored personnel carriers and head south, because there's talk of a South African invasion.

The big day is coming, please go live out your dreams now, write to your parents but don't share any details with them. No one is born a soldier, but you are already forged in steel. We're going to make those racists understand who we Cubans are."

That's what our captain will tell us prior to departure. Then he'll tell me, "Soldier Raúl, come to my tent. I have a mission for you."

He will order me to lower my pants, down to my ankles, will stick his right hand in my mouth, lubricate his penis with my saliva, and then penetrate me hard with one sole thrust.

"Don't scream," the captain will order me a day before our departure and it will be raining very lightly outside. I will clench my teeth, I've learned that in successive lives, to clench my teeth and take it, this is Cassandra's appointed fate after denying the love of a god, I feel the captain's penis perforating my insides, I hear him panting behind me, I hear him whisper: "Whore, don't let anyone find out about this."

When he's done, I feel myself drowning, I feel like I'm at home again and the checkerboard floor is turning into an ocean of parallel lines.

"We came to settle our debt with humanity," the captain repeats when we're ready to depart.

Many of the soldiers won't return: Rogelio Isidrón, a machine gunner who stands very close to me, will be executed for raping an Angolan woman and then sticking a bayonet in her neck to keep her from talking. He doesn't know it yet, he hasn't even laid eyes on that thin-waisted young woman. I see it clearly, if he would believe me, I'd tell him, "Rogelio Isidrón, please don't go to the *quimbo* on April 27, 1984."

But I know he won't believe me.

I'm very still as I listen to the captain.

I will go in the captain's jeep, I'll be his secretary by day and his bitch by night, while everyone sleeps. He'll set up a hammock for me, very close to his.

"I need him close by so he can write letters, ordinances, regulations," he'll claim when he is asked.

Then, when everyone is asleep, he'll clothe me in one of those dresses he brought from Luanda and I'll elegantly walk around the tent, barely lit by a lantern, I'll light a cigarette and I'll sing very softly so no one hears me.

"You are Camille the French girl. I've never been with a woman who so closely resembles my love back in Holguín," he'll say, and he'll seem happy. He has already killed the leopard, that's why he has the skin hung on the wall of his tent when we pick up camp and go farther south, waiting for the South Africans to get closer. We hear the noise of the Mirages' turbines flying overhead. Firebirds. They remind me of the Erinyes and how they wanted to sink their claws into us.

"The South Africans are getting closer, but we'll know how

to repel them. We have great faith in this combat unit, which has achieved glory in multiple actions."

We listen to him at attention, under the torrid sun, he crosses back and forth in front of us in his camouflage uniform, in the company of high-ranking Cuban officers and an Angolan general. We're not alone, along with us are the other units from the Fifth Division, we are five thousand men listening to the general and the commander. Tomorrow night, Silvio Rodríguez will sing, he'll come in a combat helicopter, we'll gather in the little square hastily prepared for this purpose and we'll listen to him sing, and when he's on the line that goes *if only something would happen to suddenly erase you*, the captain will look over at me and I'll feel the captain's gaze and it will feel like the heavy rucksack on my shoulders.

I will be sitting on the earth of Angola alongside other soldiers listening to the troubadour, I will hum along to his songs with the other soldiers, while the captain gazes at me with hate. He's so jealous, the captain, he thinks I could fall in love with some other soldier and go off into the bush and let him penetrate me, that's why he beats me for no reason. He dresses me like a woman and he hits me in the gut and then says it's because he loves me. The captain is going to kill me, I know it, if I wanted to, I would kill him first, but I don't want to.

"My love bothers you," Silvio Rodríguez sings under the sky of Africa dotted with stars that we inhabitants of the northern hemisphere had never seen before coming to Africa. Next to me, nearly brushing up against my arm, is a young Angolan soldier. It's strange because his uniform isn't from the FAPLA, rather, it is the dark green of the UNITA. It takes me a few seconds to realize that this soldier is not next to me, but very far away, preparing the Chinese-made mortar with which he'll kill Martínez, who is now singing loudly "My love bothers you" and moving his head from side to side along with the other soldiers in a way that looks rather ridiculous. Martínez will be the first fatality in our unit. I see the little Angolan soldier, I look at his thin, muscly arms, his wide nose and his eyes, so dark. I can't speak to him because he doesn't exist, at least not like this, sitting next to me, listening to a Silvio Rodríguez song. The only song we should sing is the one the Erinyes are chanting now. *It's unraveling, it's unraveling, it's unraveling*, the Erinyes chant, and it's a rock group that also includes a harpy, two sirens, a centaur, the Lernaean Hydra, and a chimera.

It's unraveling, they sing loudly, while Silvio continues to croon.

All of it can be summed up in one chant:

"Down with scum, down with scum, down with scum, down with scum," my father used to sing, before he found out that his son José was leaving too, like scum.

Now Silvio Rodríguez goes quiet and looks at the Cuban National TV camera. I see him frozen in time, suspended like a drop of rain that will never reach the dust. It's going to rain when the other singer who was invited steps onstage, a woman of significant girth and disheveled hair, who will take the microphone from Silvio's hands and, looking somewhere beyond us, will belt out a song with such a powerful voice that it will quiet the Erinyes themselves: a tragic, terrible song. These Erinyes were there while Agamemnon and I, over in Micenas, were walking on the carpet that was purple, the color of the gods, they were there while Clytemnestra and Aegisthus plunged their swords in my chest, watching me writhe in agony, clutching the statue of Athena. Now they watch hungrily as Sara González sings:

"We remember the heroes without tears / and they live on here . . ."

Sara González sings and the whole Cuban army moves its head from side to side, sitting on the grass in Angola, and some even grab each other's hands while they listen to her. They all think of themselves as heroes, even the most abusive ones, like Carlos, who blows a kiss at me and whispers, "Marilyn Monroe."

The Erinyes' eyes water so much that they seem to jump out of their sockets, their coarse locks stand on end and their claws become the color of grass shining under the morning dew. The song pleases them so much that they even stop their monotonous singing, but they continue sailing onward in the Cuban-made gray coffins. Coffins for us, who went off to war and are now in the thick of it, while, three hundred miles to the south of us, a column of South African tanks begins its march, and ten miles to the northeast, a little soldier with skin as black as anthracite and fleeting eyes like a panther's, whom I no longer see sitting next to me, places a mortar on his back, takes leave of his fellow soldiers, and makes his way forward through paths known only to spiders, serpents, and leopards. His steps barely graze the tree's fallen leaves. I look at Martínez, I see his arrogant Miramar smile, the gold wristwatch he wears, his hair that is almost as blond as mine, and I am glad he is enjoying what will be his last concert on this earth. Over in Cuba, his father, Esteban Martínez Olivera, an orthopedic surgeon by profession, of whom Lieutenant Martínez speaks with so much pride—especially to remind the captain and other officers that they are nothing, beings made of air, while he is descended from an illustrious family—is sitting in a varnished wooden rocking chair and reading a Gabriel García Márquez novel, the words falling like overripe plums within the brain of this doctor, who still exercises his profession, but only to operate on members of the Party's Central Committee and foreigners with good references. *Nicanor, Nicanor, Nicanor, the name by which Death knows all men*, the doctor reads without knowing what to think about it. He goes to the bathroom and when he looks at himself in the mirror, he is met by my eyes.

'm fifteen years old, I wait for my mother to bid me good night and go to sleep, saying, "Don't be up so late reading, Rauli, remember that there's school tomorrow. Heat up a glass of chocolate milk, son, you're so thin."

"Yes, Mamá."

"Do you love me, my child?"

"Yes, Mamá."

When I sense that she's asleep, I go into the room that was Nancy's and pick a short, flowered dress that I know looks very good on me, I put on the Chanel perfume and make myself up in front of the closet mirror, I put on the heels that her Bulgarian boyfriend brought her from Istanbul, patent leather shoes with a barely noticeable golden sheen, I take a purse that was also hers and that she bought in Havana the last time we traveled together, and I tuck in several pages of my poetry. I'm about to leave when I hear my mother calling me.

"Rauli, come here."

I go into my mother's room. The light is off and I can barely see the fragile, thin shape of her, covered by a quilt. She smells like Chanel.

"Are you going out, Nancy? Did you ask Papá for permission? You know it's very dangerous out there. Have a good time, little sister, but before you go, bring me a glass of water . . . and don't let it be too cold, please."

I pour my mother a glass of water and she hugs me and tells me she loves me in a low voice that is barely a whisper and then she falls asleep. I open the door. I go down the stairs dressed as a woman and the few neighbors who are still sitting on the benches in front of the building don't recognize me. I'm just an apparition to them.

"Hi," says Clara from across the street. "You must be related to the Iriartes, right? Niece?"

"Yes," I reply. "From Havana."

"You look so much like Nancy," Jorge, her husband, says. Everyone in the building calls him Fatty because he's so skinny. "Welcome to Pastorita."

"Thanks," I say.

I take the route 6 bus heading to Punta Gorda, the city's most upscale neighborhood. I get off at the sixth stop. I walk along the promenade, which is full of people at this time. My flowered dress seems to shine in the darkness of the Cienfuegos night. I feel comfortable when I dress like this and no one knows me and I can say I am Cassandra and no one will look at me funny. I'm a girl on her way to a party at Casa de la Trova. When I arrive, there in the middle of the barely lit room, sitting on a chair, microphone in hand, a tall young man with a closely shorn head is reading poetry in which there is not a single metaphor, poetry that escapes the gateway of his teeth like the souls of dead warriors fleeing the doors of Ilios. I take a look around, spy an empty chair, and sit down next to two guys, one of whom is holding a guitar over his knees. They're both wearing Russian boots even though it's the middle of summer, their feet must be burning, I think, in my nice heels. The host and director of the Trova, a short and rather round young man with long hair and glasses, and an olive-skinned girl with curls that do nothing for her, whom I will later find out is the literature consultant, come up to us with a tray full of plastic cups.

"Would you like some Russian tea?" the girl asks and, without waiting for my response, puts the cup in my hands. There are about two dozen of us young people of both sexes.

We blow on the hot tea, we drink it and we talk, or rather, they talk, I am just a girl with very blue eyes who looks German or English and whom the young men see as a possible conquest.

"What's your name?" The one with the guitar takes the lead, introducing himself as Raúl Torralba, a troubadour from Havana.

"My name is Nancy. I know a Raúl."

"Ah . . . is he a writer?" the other one says. "I'm a poet, from here, Cienfuegos, my name is Rogelio Iglesias, and I won the Provincial Prize for Literary Workshops. Do you want to listen to something of mine?"

"That's what I came for."

"Are you also a writer?"

"Yes."

"Poetry?"

"Yes."

"But you don't talk much for a girl who's so pretty. You can tell how green you are still. Have you read Wichy Nogueras?

Back in Havana, we get together with Wichy and Víctor Casaus and that fatso Raúl Rivero and drink a lot of rum and sometimes Silvio Rodríguez himself comes by, and we really get going . . ."

"Silvio told me he's taking me on his next tour, so I can get some training," the troubadour interrupts with a sharp voice.

"Does it bother you if I smoke?"

"I read a lot of César Vallejo," I say, "and . . ."

"*I will die in Paris, on a rainy day,*" the poet recites, enunciating his words, "*on some day I can already remember . . .*"

"I'm going to add some music to that," the troubadour interrupts after lighting his cigarette. He offers me one; I nod, and he lights it with a metallic lighter, looking me in the eye.

They keep talking about César Vallejo, crossing their legs like Vallejo and putting on sad Vallejo faces and, in fact, their faces are as thin and as gaunt as the Peruvian poet's in the famous photo.

There are lots of other girls in the room, Black and white, almost all of them very thin and taller than I am. When the reading starts again, I listen to verses about tractors, fishing boats, the building of schools, and love of work.

"I'm such a mess, love, I'm such a mess, love, I'm such a mess, love," whispers a blond girl with the face of a boxer and a voluptuous chest who has approached the troubadour, the poet, and me with a glass of rum in hand, without heeding the poetess at the microphone, who's shedding verses about how good it is to labor in the countryside with your classmates.

"Where did you come from?" she asks after she sits down.

"I'm from Matanzas," I say. "I came to see my aunt."

"From what part?" the troubadour asks, but before I can reply, the party's organizer comes up to us.

"Raúl, it's your turn. Give it all you've got."

The troubadour takes his guitar, walks to the chair and microphone in the center of the room, and says that the song with which he plans to regale us sprang from a night when he was walking through the Malá Strana, the famous neighborhood in Prague, and saw a girl with very blue eyes that reminded him of Alejandra, the character from the Ernesto Sábato novel.

"Eyes like hers," he continues and points at me.

The young poet sitting next to me, who at that moment was grazing my pinkie with his right hand, grumbles angrily. Everyone looks at us and I want the earth to open up and swallow me, because sitting on one of the chairs farther away from us is a math teacher who knows me from school. I see the teacher's eyes looking at mine, as if he were reading me, as if he were digging in them with a very wide shovel and finding, beneath the sands of Hellespont, that invisible Raúl, the Spineless. He doesn't say anything, he turns and looks straight ahead. I don't know if he has recognized me, but I feel unsettled and am filled so deeply with that desire for the earth to swallow me, so that I can barely manage a smile.

"I'll be right back," I tell the poet when the guitar chords begin.

"Where are you going? Aren't you going to listen to the song? Not that you'll miss much, it's crap . . ."

"I'll be right back," I repeat. I stand up and leave the Casa de la Trova while the troubadour, with a studied falsetto, belts out a song that aims to channel Silvio Rodríguez.

N ow I'm in Angola and I only dress as a woman so that the captain can dream he has visited distant palaces and found me in a haven of peace, beyond the horizon where the rainbow begins. I'm his secret paradise, sometimes he tells me so:

"I live for you, Rauli, I wake for you, Rauli, I eat and drink for you, I order the troops for you, I exist for you, Rauli."

At other times, he orders me to remove the slutty clothes and dress as what I am, a Cuban soldier, and when I take the dress off over my head, he takes me by the neck and squeezes, squeezes tight. Then he forces me to turn around and he penetrates me hard, just once, it hurts a lot and I have to bite down on my hands not to yell. After he ejaculates and I'm getting dressed, he smacks me full across the face and says, "You're sullying my glory in combat."

You can take your glory and shove it up your ass, I think, but I don't say anything. The words tire out and die. Like apathetic gods, they fall to the checkerboard floor of the palace that exists solely for the greater glory of the captain, who, when he wants to, rubs the magic lamp for the genie to appear and ask, "What is your wish, my master?"

"What do I wish? Well, turn this filthy soldier into a beautiful woman who looks like my wife over in Cuba, but also like Marilyn Monroe, Brigitte Bardot, Olivia Newton-John. And turn this horrible tent, which is hot all day and cold as death at night, into the Taj Mahal, or Versailles, where I can lose myself with my lady without anyone seeing us. Come on, genie, hurry up."

But when the captain tires of the game, the marble-and-gold walls fade away and the checkerboard floor goes back to being the Angolan earth in which Raulito's bones will rest forever. I will not return to Cuba in a vessel that is tapered at the end. My bones will remain here in the Angolan dirt. "To the heroes," Sara González sings with a face that looks scared, her voice rising with a tremble and a hint of bitterness and alarm, as if she senses the rumbling of the South African tanks advancing across the dusty slopes. Men with English and Dutch last names are coming for us, led by a general with white hair and a sinister look, assigned by Pieter Willem Botha himself to the mission of massacring anyone who speaks Spanish. And if it's Spanish spoken with an accent from the eastern part of Cuba, so much the better.

"The South African commander told his troops, 'Tell them to say *spaghetti*, and if they pronounce it *epagueti*, then you'll know to shoot 'em in the head,'" the captain tells us when we're in formation, ready to go, and of course it's a joke.

The captain doesn't waver. We're Cubans, who could go against us? If I move forward, follow me, if I stop, push me, if I go backward, kill me. The column of South African tanks moves forward, led by that fierce-eyed general who studied at West Point and never saw a Cuban in his life before today. The column moves forward along a path of spiders and serpents, of mosquitos and hyenas and leopards and monkeys that go silent as they watch it pass; from the northeast, as well, Savimbi's young soldier moves forward, carrying a 120-pound mortar that will kill Cubans. He moves forward while wearing amulets consecrated by the priest of Shango, his guardian orisha, around his neck and wrist. Martínez's fate moves forward in the shape of that young Black soldier with a mortar on his back and our own fates move forward, all the soldiers' and the captain's and mine, moving forward as the days and nights progress. We will go out into the deserted countryside to face the racist enemy tanks, steel against steel, man against man, the day approaches, the gods are with us, all the gods and the fallen warriors from numerous battles, those devoured by lions and hyenas, those beaten down by the sun's glare and the nighttime cold, those dismembered by lashings, those buried alive in diamond mines, those who saw their people leave for the Americas and never return; those who saw their people taken to Europe to be displayed in cages are with us. I see Shango, Yemayá, Obatalá, but I also see Apollo, Ares, Artemis, and Athena. We are an army of the living and the dead, and we rise one morning at daybreak and take a position that allows us to see the enemy combat vehicles, and suddenly we feel a roaring above our heads and they are MiG-21s flying south, surrounded by harpies and chimeras, followed by winged horses and by Erinyes. The day of death approaches.

"I'm not going to tell you that you carry on the legacy of our hero of independence, General Maceo, because you already know that. I'll just say this: the time to act is here, the time to prove who is a man or a cockroach," the captain says, looking at all of us, the combat team already at our backs.

We're standing on the small square, ready to board the armored personnel carriers, to the left is the Fifth Regiment of glorious combat tanks and to the right, the Eighth Battalion of glorious combat heavy artillery. We are the Sixth Battalion of motorized infantry and our glorious combat remains to be seen.

"For Martínez," the captain says, because Martínez is already dead.

"For Martínez!" all yell.

"For Martínez!" I yell, even though I never liked Martínez very much.

"To battle!" says the captain.

I'm going to board the armored personnel carrier with my squadron, but then the captain says, "Come with me, soldier Raúl Iriarte."

I get into his vehicle, alongside him, behind the driver and the artilleryman. The captain takes the radio team's microphone to his mouth and I hear him say, in a serious voice, "All units, all units, begin your march," and then the engines roar and we get moving. We're going to battle, Cassandra is going to battle, but there is no glory in this battle, just confusion, stink, and death. We are the bridegrooms of death. I am the bride of death. We will have to get out of the armored personnel carrier when the moment comes and make our way through the tall grass with the AKs ready in our hands.

"I want to kill a little apartheid soldier," the driver sings in a sharp falsetto voice.

I don't want to kill anyone, Cassandra thinks, sitting next to the captain, who is wiping the sweat from his brow with a very un-military handkerchief, but I know it's not my day and that sheds the fear from me like the skin of a reptile. For the soldier who's singing, however, it *is* his day. A shell will split the vehicle in two, when the captain and I are walking the African plains. The driver will die alone, the artilleryman will have enough time to leap into the grass. The driver is called Osmel González Izquierdo and he would have been an actor, but the fates decreed his life would be cut short here in Angola, so far away from Havana's theaters. He sings without a care now, not suspecting that it is a song of mourning. An unburied corpse, he will wander the battlefield until, many years later, he is transferred to Cuba, not in a large box tapered at the end, but a small one in which only his dust and bones can travel. A battalion moves forward through the grass, that is what we are, because we're walking with bayonets at our hips and the captain and the battalion's top brass are very close behind the scouts. Behind them are the five companies and squadrons. Behind me, because I'm going alongside the captain who carries his rifle in his hands, is Carlos, the leader of my squadron, who is not whispering "Marilyn Monroe" to me and whose eyes are wide open. My eyes are also those of a panther, and so are the captain's, and everyone's.

"Spread out!" the captain orders, and we all begin to distance ourselves from each other.

I will kill a blue-eyed South African soldier, my Zeus, I will find him in the grass and my rifle will spit out a burst of fire that will split him in two. I go to meet that soldier, just today I began dreaming of him, I saw him there on the Boer farm, shaving before the mirror, dressed only in his military pants.

Tall and awkward, with bushy eyebrows and a tired gaze, the private first class or caporal Ernest Naaktgeboren, son of a Presbyterian minister and a housewife, Led Zeppelin fan and horse lover, wanted to study at West Point but he wasn't admitted due to his extreme scoliosis. Ernest wears an amulet under his military jacket meant to protect him from the spells and bullets of the Blacks, but it won't protect him from my bullets or from the fate that will twist like the vine tangled at his feet that makes him run headlong into a stone, while his companions from the First Company of the Twenty-Sixth South African Expeditionary Infantry Battalion retreat.

"Cubans are witches," the ghosts whisper. "There's something not quite right about the Cubans," the South African women murmur over there, so far from the front as they pray to their white-people's God. "The Angolans who dress themselves in Cuban clothes become audacious, reckless, because the uniforms are bewitched," they murmur in the barracks, because the South Africans can feel the whirlwind of vengeful spirits surrounding us, all of them except you, Ernest, you who will remain hidden in the grass until after your companions have retreated and I have shot you, I won't be able to help it because the finger of Raúl Iriarte, Cuban citizen, who is, by profession, a soldier of the expeditionary infantry, will press the trigger of the AK before Cassandra can stop it.

I crouched in the tall grass, I removed his helmet, and I looked at the face of Ernest Naaktgeboren, at his rough peasant's hands sprouting blondish hair that reminded me of my father's hands, at his body, long and thin in a camouflage uniform beginning to soak through with dark blood, at his feet covered in thick-soled yellow boots. I cleaned the blood off of his face with a handkerchief and then his eyes, rolling wildly in their sockets, fell upon me, he moved his lips, said something I didn't understand, I brought the canteen close to his mouth, but before he could drink, he began to shake, even the grass surrounding him shook. I felt my comrades' steps coming closer and I didn't want them to see that I was capable of killing. So I stood up and let him die alone.

The death was attributed to soldier José Ocampo Guillén from the Third Company. That soldier carried the man I'd killed while I heard the captain calling me amid the tall grass, "Raúl, where are you?"

No one else in the unit killed a South African. Hand-to-hand combat didn't take place, the artillery battalion reactivated, the planes and tanks forced them to cross the border. A great victory.

"I killed one," the soldier José Ocampo Guillén yelled and shot three short bursts at the corpse, my corpse, Cassandra's corpse, a dead man among the high grass of the plains, dressed in the enemy's green-gray.

They will search for his papers and see that he was called Ernest Naaktgeboren.

"*Compañeros*, on this day, we can announce that we've repelled the attempted invasion by the imperialist forces of apartheid that dared to tread on sacred Angolan land," the commander in chief said over every radio wave in the world, the news even reached Olympus, and you, father Zeus, stroked your beard and thought that those Cubans were about to surpass the glory of the Spartans in Thermopolis, and, in your omnipotent vainglory, you sent us the plague of cholera and our whole division fell ill with high fevers as we returned to our base. Even the tanks and armored personnel carriers looked sick and the planes flew with their heads bowed and the Angolan and Cuban flags didn't wave with pride even though the wind was blowing steadily. I got sick, and the captain was now a major, although they still hadn't confirmed his promotion in Havana, and our battalion was now crowned by glorious combat, although we'd only killed one South African, that little soldier met with a burst of machine-gun fire, first by me, and then by José Ocampo Guillén, who was promoted to private first class and received the order of courage. We already went to meet our death, hyenas, leopards, antelopes, snakes, spiders, gods, and orishas watched us pass as they trembled, we saw the tanks, we saw the reactive artillery and the 130 mm cannons, we saw the MiGs flying overhead, we saw our battalion's heavy machine guns firing, we saw the cannons of our AK rifles pointing south, to where the South African comes from, and we saw the fire rise up on the African land and devour the world, and I saw Ares, naked, his muscular body shining, pushing aside the tall grass as we marched forward in search of a target. I saw Ares, who smiled at me and said, "Cassandra. With me by your side, who could fight against you, Cassandra?"

'm in the schoolyard, it has been raining, that's why the check-erboard floor is full of yellow almond-tree leaves and there's a pleasant smell that makes its way into my nose and makes me want to sneeze, and the bust of Martí has a black butterfly resting on his bald spot that slowly opens and closes its wings as if it had all the time in the world. I am eleven years old and a classmate has decided to hit me because I was looking at his girlfriend. I didn't particularly like his girlfriend, but it was nice to sit near her and watch how her skilled hand drew horses in her math note-book, horses with wings that took me back to Ilios and recalled the wide plains where my brother Hector taught me how to ride horseback, long before Paris turned up with Helen and brought us to our knees. The girl, svelte with swaying hips, a volleyball player, I thought, noticed me watching her and lifted the sheet to show me those palfreys running on the plains of the paper's parallel lines, and when she smiled, I smiled, just that and noth-ing else. But that was enough for her boyfriend, hairy, with rest-less legs that never stopped moving as the teacher tried to get on with the class, and he sent me a sheet ripped from his notebook that said only, "I'll see you at recess, Spineless, I'm gona cut off your dik."

I was already pretty dickless before he threatened me.

The bell rings, abrupt as a train whistle moving through the western plains. The teenagers escape the room without waiting for the English teacher to read the Milton poem.

"*And welcome thee, and wish thee long,*" the teacher says only for me, looking at me with those deep-set eyes, too big for her face, and then she picks up her files from the desk and smiles at me with limitless patience, and since I am still sitting there, looking at her, she asks, in a serious tone, "Did you like the poem?"

"Yes, teacher," I reply in English.

"You can go," she says then.

I go out to recess. Athena has promised me that she will no longer be fickle, and that she will fight alongside me. The kid is waiting for me in the middle of the play area with his hands on his hips. He's tall for his age. I'm the shortest in the class, just barely taller than a fifth grader, and we're in seventh grade. I'm no match for him and he knows it, but he's going to teach me a lesson, and the other kids, girls and boys, start to circle around us and one says, "The first one to go hits twice," and another says, "Let it all out."

"You hit him first, right there between the eyes," urges Athena, who is transfigured into the body of Obatalá. "Go."

I get close.

"Why were you looking at my girlfriend, Spineless, you piece of shit?" he asks, and his voice sounds childish, almost innocent. The youngest in the class, but also the tallest.

"She draws so nicely," I reply.

He doesn't like my reply and he hits me, hard, in the face, so hard that I fall into the dust.

"Get up, Cassandra," Athena orders and she holds out her hand to me, but I prefer to remain sitting in the dust.

"Spineless, Spineless, Spineless!" my classmates shout, and I look at Athena with intense reproach as I tell her that Cassandra was never an Amazon. When I get home, I tell my father that I got hit and stayed down, he doesn't care that I'm almost always getting hundreds or that the Spanish teacher thinks I could be a poet, it's not enough that I get top marks in gym class despite being so thin that I'm practically nonexistent. It's not enough. He wants me to be a man, and he hits me in the head with his enormous mechanic's hands, hands that seem to have little to do with his body, so scrawny when he's dressed, all muscle when he's naked. My father usually has ten eggs for breakfast in the morning before getting into his old car and kissing my mother goodbye. To my father, lacking courage is the greatest possible sin, whether you're a man or a woman. My father roars like the Nemean lion and spits like the Lernaean Hydra when he finds out that his youngest son was hit and didn't fight back. He doesn't ask where the teachers were, or anything like that. We are sitting at the dinner table, the three men in the family: my father, my brother who, even though he hates my father, agrees with everything he says, and me.

"Come on, tell me what happened," he says slowly, with a smile I know all too well as he jingles the keys to the car. Then he pours out a finger of rum for my brother and me and a double for himself, and drinks it with his eyes locked on mine.

My brother also drinks and looks at me. It's the first time I've ever drunk something so strong and it won't go down my throat, I keep it in my mouth awhile and stare at my father, who says with that hoarse voice of his, "Swallow."

I swallow and I sneeze.

"Talk," my father says and I tell him about the girl who draws and that her name is Marlene and that her bad-tempered boyfriend Joaquín pushed me to fight, and that I thought it was wrong to fight because my mother and the Russian woman . . .

"What does the Russian woman have to do with it?" my father asks, growing more and more furious.

He serves himself another drink.

"Keep going," he says.

"It's not right to fight, and less still at school," I tell him, as my mother told me, "because then they put it in my record and they screw up my future and . . ."

"Shut up already," my father says and brings his right hand to my face, so that I can see the dirty, blunt nails that look like they were cut with a machete instead of manicure scissors, the fingers that look like a giant toad's from up close.

Then he pushes back his chair as he stands up and says, "Are you a fag or what? Tomorrow, I'm going to school with you."

My brother takes a drink, looking at us, and then shrugs his shoulders. "Have fun with that," he says.

I would like to be my brother.

I go to school with my father. He's ignorant, he dropped out after ninth grade and barely made it through a mechanic's course, and he's on the small side, with dirty hands, but they respect him because his blue eyes emit a rage that practically turns him into a giant, surliness without measure. My father has the eyes of a serial killer. He arrives very early, when the kids are still waiting for school to open.

"Where is he?" he asks me.

I point at Joaquín, who is sitting with Marlene and another teenager in the doorway of one of the houses adjoining the school.

"Hey, you, come over here," my father says in a voice so loud that many of the students turn to look.

"Who, me?" the kid asks with indifference.

"Yes, you, and you show me respect. I'm not that *cabroncito* you took advantage of just because you're bigger, so it's in your best interest to stay calm and come over here."

My father looks at him so fiercely that the kid, intimidated, stands up and comes over.

"You tell your father that I want to see him here tomorrow," my father tells him. "Tell him I don't want to have to go looking for him at his house."

My father will call upon a courage I do not possess, he thinks he has to be courageous for me, a nothing. He's going to punch the kid's father, a known athletic trainer who is over six feet tall and 210 pounds of pure muscle. He will emerge victorious, as he almost always does, although with a broken nose. It will be my father's last great victory in my lifetime. Later, I will go off to Angola. Cassandra will go off to Angola, without her white dresses, and my father will be proud of his son, who won't return, and then, when I die, he will say when he remembers me that it was all over "less than an inch," because if I'd been half an inch shorter, they wouldn't have let me in the army.

'm just the remains of a soldier, dressed as a woman on this night when no one is watching the captain and me. Because I must compose the letters to the mothers of the dead, I am afforded the blessings of a married woman. To the mother of Osmel González Izquierdo, the driver of the armored personnel carrier that was split in half by a Chinese-made shell. To the mother of Raúl Isidrón, the company's anti-tank rocket launcher operator, who will no longer draw naked odalisques for his companions to masturbate to and whose forehead was pierced by the bullet of an Israeli-made rifle, leaving a large hole through his head. To the mother of Alberto Guerra, who was taken by malaria one morning when I was also delirious with fever and whom I saw fading away, since he was very close to me in the infirmary, and when he started to convulse, I saw the nurses and the doctor running toward him, but forget it, he didn't make it. To the mother of Roberto Rovira, a kid from Nuevitas whom we knew as Camagüey and who stepped on a mine and went flying through the air, who went so high up that when he came back down, he couldn't find himself. To the mothers of Lieutenants Bernardo Álvarez and José Cifuentes, leaders of the First and

Third Companies, killed by a missile that landed on a jeep driven by Bernardo. Due to the deaths of these officers, the report has to say, "The casualties were few, but significant."

"Let's take a break," the captain says, and commands me to remove my clothes.

He wants me to wear the blue dress, the one I don't like because it makes me look thinner than I am, it makes me practically invisible.

"I want you to sing for me," the captain says, because it is raining thunderously loud outside and with that rain, no one is going to come interrupt our games. "Pretend you have a microphone in hand and you're Olivia Newton-John. Sing me something nice, sing me 'Xanadu.'"

"Yes, Captain," I say.

"Don't call me Captain. Call me Cap, the way I like it."

I agree and start to sing with that voice of mine that would scare away a leopard, but he likes it. The snake of his penis starts to rise because I'm running my hands over my body and I lift my dress a little, not too much, just a tiny bit, so that I seem like a virginal girl who is hinting at more. He takes a long drink, takes off his military jacket, and hangs it on the back of the chair so that it doesn't get wrinkled. It's hot inside the tent and the captain's whole body shines with sweat and anxiety. I'm also anxious, there's something in the air that I don't like. We're being watched, I know it. The night is full of eyes, my Zeus, we're being watched. Like the son of the Christian God, soon I can say, "It is finished!" Thy will be done, my Zeus, but the captain doesn't know it yet, he thinks that this is just a moment when in truth it is eternity.

"We are fixed in marble," I tell him, ceasing to sing and pretend that I'm holding a microphone in my hands, and I look him straight in the eye, but he's not listening.

"Get into the hammock and sing from there," he says.

He is still sitting on the canvas chair, it's well into night, the light from the kerosene lamp makes each of my movements, and each of his movements, look like phantasmagoric faces, projecting our shadows on this reality that doesn't deserve us. Less than fifty yards from us is the tent where the battalion's top officers are sleeping. If I sang louder, they would hear the voice of Cassandra channeling a pop star. Channeling Olivia Newton-John.

"Dance," the captain says, and I move around the hammock like I did in the cabarets of Cienfuegos at the age of fifteen, when I dressed like a woman and went out dancing under lights that flashed on and off, like the torches that surrounded the statue of Athena when Ajax took me by my calves, tore apart my dress, and right there, in front of the statue of the goddess, raped me and sealed his fate. I dance inside the captain's tent, the gray military canvas over my head, and beyond it, the canvas of the entire African sky and its stars, which are not Spineless Rauli's stars, but Cassandra's stars. I dance and suddenly I start to convulse, I vomit a greenish phlegm and I see that another woman is dancing, also blond with blue eyes, also wearing a dress but hers is flower-print, I hear music playing loudly. *Lucy in the sky with diamonds*, the Beatles sing, and suddenly, she stops dancing, dries the sweat off her brow with a very white handkerchief, a man offers her a glass, smiling, she takes the glass to her lips, she drinks, her eyes go white, she falls to the floor and starts convulsing, just like me. I look at her sharply defined features and I recognize her, she's the woman from the photo that the captain takes from encampment to encampment, she's the woman the captain loves, my rival over in Cuba. She will die within a week, I know, but I don't say anything, I try to keep dancing and I fall in the hammock, I'm very weak, the fever left me exhausted.

We were a whole feverish army moving forward through the green hills of Africa, returning to our old encampment.

A victorious army at death's door, people cheering for us as we passed.

"Cuba and Angola!" they cried.

"What's wrong with you?" the captain says and slaps my face with his hard soldier's hand. "Do you still have a fever?"

I've ruined the captain's fun; his erect penis will not eject semen into my anus this time. He doesn't like seeing my face, which he had been watching while pretending it belonged to an Australian movie star, now it again becomes the vulgar face of a Cuban private he needs to worry about. He's furious with me. Bad days are ahead for Cassandra, I know it, he won't like being the widower of a real woman, betrothed only to me, a nobody. When the letter arrives announcing his wife's death and they ask him if he wants to take a helicopter to Luanda and from there, a plane to Havana, then from Havana to Gibara, where the burial will take place and where his inconsolable in-laws await, he will say no, what for, and for three days he won't emerge from his tent, a kind of mustachioed, black-haired, bristly Achilles.

"Leave, go to your quarters," he'll say to me, looking at the reddish ground with his eyes dulled by pain.

"Yes, Captain," I will say, without another word to console him. I will remain standing at alert before him, and for the first time, I will feel like I want to hug him rather than shoot him in the back of his skull.

"Get on out of here, goddammit," he'll say then, his eyes hard, with narrow, canine pupils.

I'll take my rifle, my gas mask, my infantry shovel, and my rucksack, and I will be back in the squadron with Carlos, who has already seen death but not his own; according to him, he had time to fire a long burst at a group of South African soldiers in retreat.

"One of these little white guys has to have bit the dust," he's telling the members of the squad who are listening to him in formation. They look at me with hate as I stand at attention before him and carry out the military salute.

"Permission, Sergeant, to join your formation."

"Marilyn Monroe came back? The squad is fucked. What were you doing for so long, girl?" he says, coming closer, putting on a feminine voice that causes the soldiers to laugh. "Answer, that's an order," he says, because I've gone quiet. "It's in your interest to speak," he says, because I am still quiet, and then I begin to speak.

"I was writing letters for the dead," I say, and this seems to strike him as a mysterious occupation, worthy of respect.

"If you have to write to mine, tell my mother that I died a hero. Don't put anything fucked up in there, because I'll rise from the grave to get you, is that clear?"

Letters for the dead, letters for the families of the dead. *Today I have the sad duty to inform you that your son, a worthy soldier of our beloved Cuban Revolutionary Forces, fell during a combat mission, honorably fulfilling his mission as an internationalist soldier. It is our great honor to have fought alongside him and his memory will live forever in our hearts.* Letters for the dead that, when they reach Cuba, will make the mothers rise from their chairs and stand with bated breath, in disbelief at that piece of paper that tells them that their sons are no longer. Letters for the dead, terrible letters that should never arrive, but that do so anyway, like a downpour, one by one, like drops of rain sneaking in through a neglected roof. The letters for the dead arrive. Who will write the letter saying I have died? No one, because my body will never appear, I won't leave Angola, the reverse tide of time will drag me out and I'll return to Ilios and be Cassandra once again. I will again become entwined with nothingness. Can you hear the tremendous, dark silence of the gods? Can you? Then you are neither living nor dead, you're suspended in that gelatinous mass that we call Empyrean; that's me now, floating in nothingness, undertaking my return to Ilios, where I will resume my place in Hecuba's womb and become again that woman most abhorred by the gods, I will again be Cassandra the mad, believed by no one, I will go back, yes, but now I'm in the schoolyard clutching my stomach because they've hit me again. They know how to hit, they sink their fists into you, and you feel how the other person's flesh melds into your own, and then when you fall, they spit in your face and call you Spineless and that "Spineless" is like an announcement, an order, so that they all begin to shout. Apollo is among them, visible only to me, disguised as Shango he looks at me and shouts, "Spineless!"

And then the math teacher comes along: "Children, please, can't you keep it down?"

"Spineless over here is being fresh," Ernesto says.

"His name isn't Spineless," Carmen says. She is the only one who complains when they hit me, and she's the one who went to get the teacher. "His name is Raúl."

"Get out of here," the teacher says. "I can't believe this behavior. You're too grown-up for this, you bullies."

"He was asking for it. He's a counterrevolutionary," Juan Carlos says with a smile. "He was reading a forbidden book."

"So? You listen to rock and roll," Carmen says.

"That's not forbidden. You stay out of it."

"You stay out of it, you stay out of it, *you* stay out of it, you bully. Teacher, he was the one who kicked him first, ask Isabel."

Isabel nods. "Yes, teacher, Rauli hadn't done anything and Juan Carlos started to call him Valentine and Rauli stuck his tongue out at him and for that . . . well, you can see, he punched him in the stomach, he fell to the floor, and then everyone came down on him, all of them shouting, 'Spineless, Spineless!' I felt very bad for him, I even felt like crying. These boys are awful."

I watch them talking from the floor. I can't make up my mind to stand up.

"Silence! You're not his lawyer!" the teacher says. "Come on! Everyone back to the classroom. Recess is over. You're all punished, and don't let me find out that this bullying is still going on!"

When they go into the classroom, the math teacher holds out her hand to me and helps me to my feet.

"You're going to have to stand up for yourself. A young revolutionary has to know how to stand up for himself, especially when he's the smallest kid in the class. Maybe it's nothing, but perhaps you do something that makes them treat you this way, Raulito. What is it?"

"I don't know."

"You're a know-it-all. Rein it in a little, let the others answer too . . . I know you read books and that's very good for you, but leave them at home. Here almost everyone plays sports, and some are dumb as rocks, and they pick on you because of it."

"Yes, ma'am."

I enter the classroom with her, I sit down at my desk and move my feet as I listen to her say we should respect each other.

"But Raúl isn't a revolutionary," says Ariel, a boy who is almost as small as I am and almost as thin, but very jittery. "Fags can't be revolutionaries."

Laughter in the classroom. The teacher looks at me and sighs. "Who says Raulito is homosexual? He's only ten years old, and you're all barely old enough to wipe your own asses, let alone know what a homosexual is. Do you want me to tell your parents? Do you?"

Silence overtakes the classroom. No one wants that, not even me.

Me less than anyone.

We will hear the dead again, will hear them fluttering over our heads like reckless birds but the others can't see them clearly, only I can hear them, I out of everyone in our unit, I see them look at me as they turn in their endless whirlwind, Achilles close to Heracles with his cudgel, Heracles close to the great Zulu king Shaka and a Napoleonic general whose eyes teared up when he heard that part about *soldiers, from these walls, three hundred centuries watch over us,* the general alongside a young Bantu warrior who preferred death to becoming a slave, he swallowed his own tongue in front of the Portuguese who were already dragging him to the boat that would take him to the Americas, King Shaka by Ajax Telamonius, Ajax Telamonius by Ajax of Locride, Ajax of Locride by an Egyptian pharaoh, Kheops by a woman raped by the South Africans, a beautiful woman who looks at me with sad eyes, that woman standing by my brother Hector who doesn't answer me when I call to him without opening my mouth, I call to my brother Hector solely with my eyes as he leaves, hanging his head in shame for not having known how to protect Ilios.

The whirlwind of dead souls like dark storm clouds above us.

We have to placate the dead, an offering is needed, that is why we killed the leopard.

"We'll take care of it," the captain says and goes out very early in his jeep, accompanied by Martínez, Lieutenant Amado, and Carlos, carrying their AKs and a rifle with a scope.

They buy a pig in the village and tie it to a tree to attract the leopard. They will come back two days later and drop the leopard's corpse in the middle of the little packed-earth plaza where the battalion meets, all to placate the dead. But they do not know that's what it's for, they think they are obeying the invocations of the village's prominent members, they don't know that behind the leopard's death there are ancient deaths, so old they're a blur to me. My mother Hecuba is there, although she doesn't want me back, she wants me alive, even if it's in the fleeting form of Spineless Raulito.

R ead it," he said to me, and I reread the part where it says, *Comrade Captain, it is your duty to be strong, because the Fatherland and the Revolution and the children of the Fatherland under your care all need you. We are sorry to inform you that three days ago, your young wife Katerina Rodríguez Morales suffered acute poisoning after consuming a crème liqueur mistakenly made with methanol. The members of the medical team at the Provincial Hospital of Holguín made every effort to save her, but nothing could be done. She died, cared for until the very end.*

When I finished, he asked me to read it again, and when I read the part where it said she died, his eyes teared up again. He hugged me and repeated that I looked like her and then he hit me hard in the stomach because I am not her. I was left doubled over on the floor, covering my head with both hands in case the captain thought to strike me again. I am starting to like it when he hits me like that, viciously, without stopping. His wife has died, she died while we were a battalion of shadows coming back from a victorious dawn, she died in Cuba, in Holguín, where nothing should have befallen her, while the whirlwind of the dead was asking us for human sacrifices, Agamemnon first among them. She died so that the fevers would stop and not another soldier would be killed, but I can't tell him that. I wasn't with him when a lieutenant, sent on express orders from the division's top brass, whose uniform seemed black in that Angolan evening, looked into the captain's eyes and handed him the letter and told him to read it right then in front of him, but to sit down first and to be strong, a real Cuban man, a macho in all senses of the word, because moments like these are the true tests of men.

"Have a drink," the lieutenant insisted, "go on, the strongest rum you have."

The lieutenant, tall, dark-skinned with a baritone voice, took pleasure in listening to himself as my captain calmly opened the bottle of Havana Club that he saved for special occasions, calmly brought out those two etched glasses that were gifted to him by a captain of the Portuguese army, calmly poured in the rum, calmly sat down, calmly looked the lieutenant in the eye for almost five seconds, and then calmly slit open the envelope and began to read. I had gone with two other soldiers to the division's central warehouse, located a little over a mile from the battalion's headquarters, but I heard the scream that, like a dark wind, went knocking the leaves from trees, scaring off birds and monkeys, breaking apart cobwebs, making hyenas howl and the antelope raise its head before the lion could approach, a scream that reminded me of Achilles's weeping at the death of Patroclus . . . We are but shadows set on the canvas of this life, my Zeus, I thought as I listened to the hoots of the hyenas and the wild dogs, watched as the entire Cuban army came to a halt at the captain's muffled scream, which remained fixed in his pain and ended everything for him and for me.

You feel night falling, you feel the power of the night as a priceless good when you can at last be alone with yourself, hidden away in the false protection of your hammock. When you don't have to listen to Carlos, who says, "You must have done something for the captain to send you here . . . You probably threw yourself at his cock. You can't go doing that, Marilyn Monroe. I promise I'll make a real soldier out of you."

Agustín, lying on the hammock next to me, hands me back my copy of *Anna Karenina*.

"I took care of it for you so they wouldn't grab it to wipe their asses. I liked it well enough, but not as much as Malcolm X."

That book, *The Autobiography of Malcolm X*, is Agustín's favorite, which he brought from Cuba. It's a kind of Bible for him, like *The Iliad* is for me. Agustín hasn't read *The Iliad*, so I offer it to him since I know it practically by heart.

"No," he says, "it's written in verse, and I'm not going to understand a thing. Better for you to tell me about it."

I sit on the hammock and begin, "*Sing, Goddess, Achilles's rage, / Black and murderous, that cost the Greeks / Incalculable pain, pitched countless souls / Of Heroes into Hades's dark . . .*"

I try to talk low, so that Carlos doesn't come back in and punish us for talking after the order to be silent. First Johnny the Rocker wakes up, then Matías, and then the entire tent is listening to the story of my brother Hector's feats and the treachery of the Achaeans, because I recount *The Iliad* my own way. I tell them about the beauty of the city's women, about the games and the horse races. I tell them about my father's palace and about how Apollo vomited in my throat because no one believed me.

"It's like going to the movies," says someone's voice from the hammocks to my right.

"Marilyn Monroe knows so much," Matías says.

"He's mad smart," another soldier says.

Perhaps you will punish me even more than you have already, my Zeus, for revealing the secrets of your children, but they couldn't seal my mouth, or they didn't want to, because although Athena, Aphrodite, and Apollo were sitting next to me in the hammock, dazed, listening to me, I was speaking to the Cuban soldiers, I told them about the deceptions, about your children's malevolence, as false as clay coins. I felt happy, my Zeus, until Fermín suddenly said to me, "That's enough of those lies. We're all Marxist-Leninists here."

He turned on the light and the magic slipped away into the African night.

We went quiet.

I lean my head against the pillow, but the words remain alive inside of me, the words take me back to Ilios and I see myself running on the sands of the beach, along with two of my sisters, and I can make out a cloud too close to the sea. It's the sail of a vessel approaching. Then more and more and more appear.

"Let's go back," I say to my sisters.

I've returned to my squadron, but the captain hates me, he only calls me in to reread the letter to him and then he hits me, hard, quick, and strong, with his ex-boxer's fists. I'm afraid he'll tell others about us.

"My good name depends on your silence," he says to me,

looking at me with his dead fish eyes. "You knew she had died and you didn't say anything to me."

"How could I know?"

"You know everything, Raulito, and you knew about her death with even more power, more conviction. I could tell in your eyes that you knew, I don't know how, but I could tell when I kissed you, you knew that she had died, when I entered you, you knew that she was no longer in this fucked-up world of the living, this damned valley of tears . . . I don't know how, but you knew and you didn't prepare me, you didn't say anything to me. That's why I hate you, and because you look like her, but you're not her. Now go back to your company."

Punishment detail in the middle of Angola, which means punishment detail in the middle of nowhere. Carlos hands me a shovel and orders me to dig a very large hole and then refill it.

"Put on your gas mask," he says. "I'm going to make you a man."

"Leave him alone, Carlos . . ." Agustín begins to say.

"What do you think," Carlos says, "that this is a little game? I'm the one who gives orders in this squadron. Soldier Raúl Iriarte does not have the necessary combat ability to be part of this company and it is my duty to get him into shape, so you shut up, because I will not hesitate to accuse you of insubordination. I don't want to hear another word from you. And you, Raúl Iriarte, get going, it's time."

I obey, I put on the gas mask that barely lets me breathe and I grab the infantry shovel.

"The captain asked me to be especially hard on you," Carlos whispers, on all fours next to me. "I don't know what you did."

On my knees, I dig a hole in the dried-up, compacted earth.

The other soldiers look at me. It's two in the afternoon and the sun is at its apogee.

"She's prettier than the one I have at home, even sweaty and all," Fermín says and everyone except Agustín laughs.

"Yeah, but no one comes here to be pretty," Carlos says, feigning seriousness. "You come here to fulfill your duty to the fatherland, and now we're a decorated unit. What happens if they come to inspect us and see what kind of specimens we've got in our squadron?"

"It's not his fault," Johnny the Rocker says in a voice that borders on a whine. "It's the fault of whatever idiot deemed this little tin soldier fit for the army."

I dig and don't look at them. Their words glide over my head and don't touch me, I'm digging a very big hole, I could almost exit through it to the other side of the earth. Athena is helping me. I'm digging the grave where they will bury my body after the captain kills me. I'm digging it as if I'm crafting a house with oak doors and invisible gardens. I dig my own grave and Athena digs it with me, I see her shoveling earth and placing it next to me with a smile on her perfect face, as empty as a bronze mask.

I f Laocoön had not struck his spear into the belly of the horse, everything would be different, they would have heard the rumbling of the Achaeans' weapons and that pop would not have silenced the whispers, those whispers that I wanted my father to hear.

"They're inside," I said, grabbing my father's arm with such force that my nails dug into him.

"Inside where?" my father asked, pretending he hadn't understood me.

"You already heard Laocoön," I insisted. "They're inside that fake horse made of wood."

"Don't be so rough, daughter," Hecuba said. "Let go of your father."

I wanted to be persuasive: "Don't you see that the horse doesn't fit through the city gates? Let's leave it here on the plains, as an offer to Poseidon."

My father, my poor father, so devoted and naïve at the same time, my poor father looked at me like he didn't see me. "How can you suggest that we leave it outside if it's an offering to Poseidon? What would the god think if we left his horse to the mercy of outlaws and thieves? Look, daughter, the Achaeans are no longer here, you can't even make out a candle on the horizon. Nothing. They're not here, they've gone. We'll open a gap in the wall so that this magnificent steed can enter, and then there will be a party in Ilios, and I will dance with you, my daughter. Unfurrow your brow, Cassandra, it mars the beauty of your face. Come."

I looked at the colossal, crude wooden horse. Laocoön's spear still shook amid its planks. I approached it and placed my hand on one of its thighs, damp with salt, its limbs carved from the remains of the ships that my brother Hector had torched. Inside were the Achaeans and everything was lost for Ilios. I wanted to speak again, but then Helen put her arm around my shoulders.

"Come on, Cassandra, this is no place for a young woman," she said with that repulsive, caressing voice, and she dragged me far from my father and I followed her, like a lamb, I followed her, I followed Helen, I entered the city through the oak doors, a crowd of young boys followed us, pretending they were Hector, but some pretended they were Achilles and were killing us in battle. I turned around and looked at the horse again, I pushed Helen's hand from my shoulders, but the gates closed behind me and the sentinels looked at me with their arms crossed.

"The game is over," they said.

I'm seventeen years old and it's six days before my birthday and I go out into the Cienfuegos night, wearing cropped pants and, tucked into them, a Russian cotton dress that I bought at the variety store. I change my outfit at my friend Roberto's house because his parents have gone to Miami and he has the house to himself until his sister returns from Varadero. It's a very old wooden house and it's full of ghosts that watch Roberto and me as we go to his parents' old room with its enormous mirror and change our outfits, hysterical with laughter. Jealous specters that watch us as we beat each other with pillows, jump on the full-size bed, and listen to ABBA on the radio, singing *chiquitita dime por qué*, and we put on makeup, feeling like a couple of happy girls. Roberto also dresses like a woman. He's twenty but looks ten years older, he's scared, he looks at me with pupils misted over by fear. It's his first time, so he's very worked up.

"*Ay*, if they realize it, they'll kill us," he says and grabs my hands in his, too big to be feminine.

"You do look like a girl," he says when we are dressed as women. We are in his living room, surrounded by pictures of his grandparents and great-grandparents, who are now the ghosts that condemn us. "No one will recognize you. Me, on the other hand . . ."

"Don't be scared," I tell him, "but don't talk, because you have quite the deep voice. If they hear us, they'll break us in two. So don't talk."

"Okay, I'll pretend I'm mute."

"Don't look at anyone's crotch. No woman does that," I tell him so that he doesn't lower his neck like a charmed gazelle, entranced and agog, when the dancers shake their genitals near him, because we're going out dancing and it's my last day in Cienfuegos. Tomorrow, I'll be on a truck headed toward Loma Blanca, where they'll get me ready to go to Angola, they'll make a tin soldier out of me. It's my last day as a civilian and Roberto and I are going to a discotheque to dance under the strobe lights. The lights take me back to Ilios, I swirl around, give a half-turn, spread my arms, and swirl while looking at the ceiling, and I become someone else. I become Cassandra in my linen clothing and I'm already at the foot of the statue of the goddess, enveloped by the smoke of the incense, feeling the heat of the fire on my face, the aroma of the sacrificial lambs, and I can hear that language that I only understand when I am sleeping.

"Cassandra, Cassandra, wake up," my mother says to me when I dance. "You're shaking, my child."

I'm shaking because I see myself in an unknown place, very far from Ilios, I'm a man who dresses as a woman and goes to a party in a place where this is very dangerous, because if anyone finds out what I am, they'll kill me. No one can suspect we have penises. No one.

"If they suspect it, we're dead, and our death will not be sweet. They will lynch us like they did Farah María, then they'll say we threw ourselves at them," Roberto says. "Remember to call me Magalí."

I'm Nancy.

Magalí and I walk along the cobblestoned streets of Cienfuegos, swaying our hips, but not too much. Our heels make a *tock-tock* sound in the early evening. We're very serious. Pretty girls don't smile too much, they cross their arms and look haughtily at some unspecified place between the sky and the earth. It took me months to get Roberto to handle heels, but now he wears them almost better than I do, although I can feel his elbow trembling in my hand. People stare at us. *She goes with all the gear, / with hoop, bucket, and shovel.*

"Let's get a taxi," Magalí says, because even though there are only ten blocks to go, she's very intimidated. Since it's Sunday, there are a lot of people on the street and they all pay attention to us, too much attention. A man passing on a bicycle turns around and says to me, "*Adiós,* Blondie."

"Where are we going to find a taxi now?" I ask Magalí. "Please keep walking, it's not much farther."

We arrive. The dance club is called Xanadu and women don't have to pay to enter. A fat man lets us in, he's wearing a tight white guayabera shirt and he looks at us without smiling.

"Come in," he says to us.

The place is full. The multicolored lights explode in our faces. "You've entered Xanadu, where everything is possible," someone says over the speakers, then Olivia Newton-John's voice starts singing the song from the movie *Xanadu.*

"What does *Xanadu* mean?" Magalí asks as we cross the dance floor toward the bar. Here, she feels more protected, because the lights blink on and off, keeping anyone from telling who's who.

"It was the Mongol emperor's palace," I tell her.

"You know everything," she says.

"Not everything."

We get to the bar and a tall, bald bartender with a cardsharp's smile asks us, "What are you dolls having?"

"Beer," I say.

"A mojito," Magalí says.

Olivia Newton-John music for men who will soon go off to war, because Cuba is at war, far, far away, in Angola. I'm also going to war but I'm not a man, I'm a petite blond lady who, sitting in her seat, with her back to the bar alongside a tall dark-haired woman, is watching the men and women move on the dance floor. Then someone sits down next to me and whispers in my ear, "You're Wendy, and your little friend is Captain Hook. She just needs a patch over her eye and a hook for a hand."

I turn around. He's a very young, thin *mulato* with the face of a champion, who, when we get to talking, ends up being a well-known boxer, a member of the national team, who is also going on a trip, not to Angola, but to Finland.

"Do you want to drink anything else?" he asks, and before we reply, he's already ordering another mojito for Magalí and beers for me and for him. The bald bartender uncaps the bottles and goes to place them on the table just like that, but the young boxer demands a glass for me, since I'm a lady.

"Where are your manners?" he says, shooting a serious look at the bartender, who apologizes, places a blue glass in front of me, and prepares Magalí's mojito.

"To your health!" the boxer says, and drinks.

We also drink. On the dance floor, couples dance to the beat of Los Van Van. *Báilalo . . . / Compóntela tú / Como el buey cansao* can be heard over the speakers and people move so awkwardly and in such a funny way that Magalí and I can't help but laugh.

"So, besides being pretty, what else do the two of you get up to?" the boxer asks, putting one of his robust hands on my left thigh, which is covered by the dress. I move his hand away while making eye contact.

"I'm sorry," he says.

"It doesn't matter," I tell him. "She's a nurse and I'm in high school."

Magalí is very serious, she's afraid again. The fact that this young boxer, upon the mere sight of her, said that she looks like Captain Hook has left her frozen, full of doubt, she feels he is on the verge of discovering the deception, and that this dance club of happy men and women will turn into an inferno of kicks and shouts. "Fags!" they'll yell if they discover us, until their voices go hoarse, and then we'll go to the police station to make a statement, bleeding and covered in bruises, and in the end, we'll go straight to that part of jail that everyone in Cuba knows as *la patera*, where they throw together the homosexuals, transvestites, and hermaphrodites. Magalí's hand near mine is shaking, I'm her only shield and safety, I'm the one who looks like a woman, and the boxer brushes up against my left hand.

"Do you want me to read your palm?" he asks.

I remain staring into his eyes, which are a deep gold color, almost black, and his face with its sharp nose, unexpected for a boxer.

"If you let me read yours later."

"Okay, I'll go first."

He takes my right hand, caresses it, and kisses the palm. I've stolen some Alicia Alonso perfume from my mother and slathered it on my palms, elbows, and behind my ears, so it's not surprising that he says I smell so good, but then he takes on the hollow, somber voice of an older man.

"You're very sensitive, Nancy, a spectacular gal, the best. When you finish high school, you're going off to Havana to study for a degree in art history, you'll graduate and then have two kids, twins, and you'll buy a house in Miramar. Things will go well for you in life, I can see it clearly, clear as day, right here in the palm of your hand."

He says it so very seriously, looking into my eyes, and the

dancing lights make his skin purple, then red, then blue, then yellow.

"Now it's my turn," I say and take his hand.

I shouldn't have done this. He's going to die very soon, in a plane crash. I feel the tightness in my chest that he'll feel when the plane begins to descend and he understands what awaits him. He will want to pray but the words won't flow out of his mouth. But right now he is looking at me with a broad smile and I smile, too, what can you do? We are just figures fixed on this canvas that you, the gods, are always painting, my cruel Zeus.

"Is everything okay, Nancy? Am I going to be an Olympic gold medalist?"

"No, silver," I say as I watch him lose his last fight against a huge Yugoslavian.

"Well, that's good enough for me," he says. "Let's go dance and let Captain Hook wait for us here."

"That's no way to treat a lady," I say patiently, and drink a sip of the warming beer.

"I say it with affection—she's actually quite beautiful. I'm waiting for a friend who does karate, who likes very tall women. He should be here any minute now . . . Let's go."

We go to the center of the floor and dance. Tomorrow, I'm leaving for Loma Blanca and from there, to Angola, today is my last day in Cienfuegos and I dance, dressed as a woman, hugging a boxer as Roberto Carlos sings *comenzó esta música suave . . . , qué bien si esta música suave no terminara jamás.* From her spot at the bar, I see Magalí watching me with a long face, looking like a sad bird. Months later, when I'm in Angola, a truck driver will give her such a beating that she'll spend three weeks in the hospital, and she'll send me a letter that I'll never be given because the glorious soldiers of Angola can't receive letters written by homosexuals. The letter will remain in the office of a robust postal employee, a member of State Security, who will issue a directive to investigate soldier Raúl Iriarte, but when they finally come to investigate me, I'll already be sailing over the dark waters of the river Styx, I'll be nothing more than a handful of dust and the wisps of grass that draw signs into the African dust, I will be waiting, like an old woman with troubled dreams, for the universe to turn over on itself and take me back to Hecuba's womb so I can be born again in Ilios of the twelve gates. That is what you have asked of me, Zeus, you've come into the hole where I lie, the tomb I dug so the captain could bury our secret, and under the assumed form of a welcome breeze cooling off my dead forehead, you've asked me to tell what I lived while I was a little tin soldier they called Marilyn Monroe. "Tell it," you said to me, and I obey you, my Zeus, how could I refuse? I'm weaving together my memories. I let them flow through my head that is nothing more than a bit of dust in the African earth. How many eons have gone by?

I go back to see the Russian woman. My father is not there. Lyudmila opens the door, gives me a kiss on each cheek, and puts the samovar on. We sit on the sofa while the tea brews and first she talks to me about life amid the birches in central Russia, then she goes to the room that serves as her library and returns with several books and speaks to me of Boris Pasternak, Vladimir Mayakovsky, Anna Akhmatova, Virgilio Piñera, José Lezama Lima. She speaks slowly to me, looking into my eyes, as if she were bequeathing to me something very beautiful. The Russian woman is so eloquent that I can see those white, cold cities, paved with pain, blood, and beauty. Listening to her, some Lorca verses come to mind: *The two rivers of Granada, / one of tears and one of blood.* Everything is like that, I think, nothing and no one are as they should be. The day before, I bought two books: Rafael Alcides's *Agradecido como un perro* and Eliseo Diego's *Antología poética.* I shouldn't have read them, my Zeus. When I read them, I understood how difficult it would be to leave this body, this life. It was painful for me to dive into those poems that were like sad music.

"You have to read Fernando Pessoa," the Russian woman says.

Lyudmila is opening herself up to me and I get lost in her outrageously blue eyes, she is the most beautiful woman I've ever seen in my life and I don't know how she can love my father, that tiny man who comes in knocking things about like a white chimpanzee, looking at us in fury because we're talking about forbidden literature.

"They warned me about you," he tells the Russian woman. "They told me you're not like the other Russians, that I have to be careful with you, that you snuck into Cuba on the sly. I accepted you, but don't you start perverting my son, because I'm not going to allow that. Is that clear?"

"I'm not perverting anyone," the Russian woman says, offended, and my father seems like he is about to hit her, I can see them clearly in my memory: a diminutive man with arms as thick as tree roots, standing on tiptoes, facing a very tall, thin woman. If the Russian woman were my mother, I would look for the knife again, but the Russian woman doesn't need me to defend her, she knows how to neutralize my father with just one disdainful look and a sharp word more cutting than ten knives.

"Drunk," the Russian woman says.

My father sinks into a chair and says, "Put on those . . ."

He was going to say "put on those Blacks," but the Russian woman doesn't allow racism in her house and he has to control himself. The Blacks are Kool & the Gang and Earth, Wind & Fire, my father's favorite bands, which he listens to until the point of ecstasy, especially when he's drunk like today, coming home enraged and perfumed with that persistent smell of alcohol.

I get up and turn on the Philips record player my father received as a gift after fixing a '57 Cadillac. My father practically shouts as he sings, trying to imitate Kool's voice. The Russian woman watches him move his hips and so do I, from the rocking chair, and the Russian woman whispers to me that he reminds her of a little Bolshoi dancer.

"Or like a poor copy of Toshiro Mifune," the Russian woman smiles, gazing at my father with tired, nearly infinite disdain. Then my father sits down and, looking at me, says again and as always:

"Just think, it was all for a measly inch."

"Wasn't it less?" the Russian woman asks.

"It's all the same, but the guy from the High Command told me that if he was just half an inch shorter, not more than that, there would be no army for Rauli."

Thanks to less than an inch, I think sometimes, I'm here in Angola, waiting for my own death—forgetting that my death was written in the book of days, that it was up to the Erinyes to decide, and here they come with their sharpened bronze dagger, toward the thread dangling from the void, my thread, and they whisper among themselves:

"You're leaving, Cassandra, it's your turn."

But that time, before my father arrived, the Russian woman was talking to me about literature. She knows a lot about Cuban poets, the Russian woman. She even knows a Lezama Lima poem.

"*O, how you escape in the moment / in which you'd already achieved your best definition / O, dear girl,*" the Russian woman was reciting to me before my father knocked at the door and heard her.

My father only reads crime novels in which there's usually a detective who's as much of a drunk as he is. He goes to the kitchen and pours himself a tall glass of vodka, adds some lemon, and sits down again, this time next to the Russian woman. He puts his arm around her shoulders and repeats hoarsely, "All over less than an inch."

My father suspects I won't return from Angola alive, he's old for his age, you can tell, especially in his eyes, weepy like a sad dog's. I would have liked to have been my father's daughter, then I wouldn't have to wear olive green, learn how to use a rifle, board a ship and go all the way off to the borders of the Old World. If I were a real girl, I would hug my father and he would console me about the difficulty of life, but instead I have to go off to war, and, even though the Russian woman once again recites, in a low voice, *O, how you escape*, my father doesn't say anything. I hear him sigh, a sigh that seems to come from a place far beyond the place my father takes up in the chair. In a little while, I will go back home, to my mother, I'll dress up as a woman and I'll sit on the checkerboard floor of my room that will then again become the wavy sea along which the ships advance upon Ilios. On that floor, my brother and I played jacks, when he still tolerated me, when it rained and he couldn't go out to play with his friends.

One night, the captain sets aside the book he was trying to read as a cure for insomnia, he sits on the hammock and sniffs at the aroma of African summer. Stealthy as the leopard whose pelt hangs on the tent's thick canvas wall, he puts on his uniform and boots and goes outside and again sniffs at the night punctuated by stars. From some point in the void, a distant smell must reach him, because he goes himself to the battalion's siren and sounds the combat alarm. It's eleven at night. We quickly put on our boots and go running out to the training area. There, standing at the center, the captain's lone figure awaits us. He is still hunting for that smell that he can't quite locate, because it's the scent of a woman who died in Cuba. We fall into formation before him.

"Attention, soldiers!" he yells, and rage floods out of his every pore.

He analyzes the companies, the platoons, the squads, one by one, he inspects the officers and the soldiers barely lit by the mercury lamps, he inspects me, my cheeks that require no shaving, my boots, my uniform, my weapons, without saying a word to me, and when he is done inspecting it all, he goes back to the center and shouts in a furious voice, "Battalion three of the mechanized infantry, to the moonlight!"

The officers look at him, perplexed. The battalion's chief of staff, First Lieutenant Argimiro Cuesta, stands before him and utters a "But, Captain" that echoes through everyone's silence.

"You stay here, Argimiro, with the sentinels," the captain stipulates in a serious tone. "The rest, follow me."

We have to plunge into the sea of dry grass that is the savanna, looking for the moonlight of the captain's revenge, the captain for whom killing UNITA guerrillas is a way to escape his pain.

The division's leadership is unaware that the Third Battalion of the mechanized infantry is going out into the night.

We advance.

"He's going to get us killed, the son of a bitch," Carlos whispers so we can hear him. He thinks it hurts me to speak ill of the captain, and he looks at me with intense hatred, as if I were responsible for the fact that the furies grabbed the officer, who is sniffing at the wind like it is going to reveal where the UNITA guerrillas are hiding.

Like little toy soldiers scattered by a naughty boy, we plunge into the places where the leopard hid when it returned from its hunt, sated by the meat stolen from the villagers. The captain advances, preceded by the scouts who open a path in the grass with strikes of their machetes. There could be a land mine hiding anywhere, we think. Around us, solitary trees waving tall, lush tops watch as the Cuban battalion, company after company, continues to plunge into the shadows.

"Nobody knows their land better than they do. They're going to make mincemeat of us under mortar fire," Carlos whispers.

"Stay alert. I'll personally fuck up anyone who stays behind. No one cough, or say a word, and I'm talking to you especially, Marilyn Monroe."

Each one of us leaves behind a trail of flattened grass. We arrive at a path at the edge of a dried riverbed.

"A goddamn elephant watering hole," Sergeant Carlos whispers, looking around as if expecting a giant elephant to come trumpeting out, its tusks held high.

A million eyes watch the troop of Cubans who are now walking the path, waiting for the captain to determine where to pin down that moonlight shining on our heads.

It's daybreak by the time one of the scouts returns to whisper something to the captain, and it's that he saw lights, just barely, glimmering in the bush. The captain picks a soldier from each company, he picks me, because he wants someone to kill me.

"When you hear the shots, advance," he tells the others.

We follow the scout. The light is waiting for us. If I concentrate, I can see five men, thin, almost skeletal, sleeping on the floor of a hut, covered by a motley-colored blanket. Outside, another man looks out into the night as if seeking something, he's a *mulato* whose father is Portuguese and his eyes are mud-colored, he's a man from the city and the night scares him, but he lights a cigarette as his companions sleep. The captain's bullet severs his brain in half, just when he was thinking he should have gone to Porto instead of staying in this country that looks more like a wasteland each day. We capture the other ones alive. Except one, into whose belly Johnny the Rocker plunges his bayonet several times. That one will go from sleep to death without noticing, almost happily, because he is as drugged as the others, who let themselves be tied up without offering any resistance. One of them says in a Portuguese we barely understand:

"*Não faça nada para nós, companheiros cubanos, nós não UNITA, nós FAPLA.*"

But they are enemies. You can tell by the quality cloth of their uniforms and their Israeli weapons. The one who spoke looks at me, thinking I'm the leader, perhaps because my skin is the lightest.

"Let's kill them," Johnny the Rocker says when the lieutenants directing the companies arrive along with Carlos, the commanding sergeant of my squad.

"None of that," the captain says and brings his flashlight up to the faces of each of the three skinny guerrillas. "Handcuff them."

Johnny the Rocker, Matías, and Carlos take the handcuffs that the captain removes from the rucksack on his back and immobilize the Angolans, who remain seated on the floor. One of them trembles as if he had a fever. They remind me of an old etching in my elementary-school history book: Black men kneeling with their arms behind them as they looked up at their captors with pleading expressions.

The captain peeks in the door.

"Don't be careless. Inspect the perimeter," he says.

"We already did," the company's leader says. "We established a tiered defense system in case you want to recover the objective."

Daybreak comes. One of the prisoners is sobbing quietly and a sordid kind of depression begins to wash over me, a desire for everything to end. I see Johnny with his bayonet still in hand, then he exits the hut and from within we can hear the unmistakable sound of retching.

I saw how the captain lifted his weapon and pointed with utmost care at that red firefly that seemed destined to disappear from one second to the next. Both of us knew that behind that little light was the face of a man taking a cigarette to his mouth, without suspecting that the Erinyes had already snapped his thread.

I saw him fall.

'm watching the sea that stretches out into the distance, the sea of Cienfuegos that is so calm it looks like a painting. In some other apartment, someone is singing a song that is more wailing than music, a plaintive monotone that has drawn me out of bed and brought me to sit on the balcony to contemplate the Caribbean and think. I'm leaving for Angola, I just turned eighteen and I have my last pass before the voyage, a special pass they gave me so I could really think about it:

"If you say no, no one will accuse you of being a wimp. The thing is, you're very small, hardly a speck," Lieutenant Bermúdez said to me. He was the political officer for the unit where I'd completed boot camp, before I received the letter of safe passage authorizing me to spend one last week in Cienfuegos.

"I'll go, I'm not afraid," I said in barely a whisper.

No one can escape his fate. It's María who is singing in the apartment on three, her husband left her and she's very sad. "The door closed at your back / and you never returned," she croons, out of tune. She is going to set herself on fire, a very common practice among Cuban women, dear father Zeus, you need alcohol, a match, and a whole lot of sadness. She won't die, she'll end up disfigured forever, she is twenty-three years old and she's singing sadly, shouting for all the building's neighbors and maybe for everyone who lives in the Pastorita complex to hear, which is a paradox, given that her husband used to beat her hard in the face and all over her body, just like what used to happen to my mother.

I used to defend my mother.

We have Savimbi's little soldiers on their hands and knees on the dirt floor of the hut. Very close to the one Johnny the Rocker killed, there's an 82 mm mortar. The sun is rising, but the captain goes up to each one of them and inspects their arms, looking for the burn marks that will give away the artilleryman. None of the survivors have them, so he approaches the deceased and looks at his arms.

"The son of a bitch who killed Martínez is dead," he says.

We return, and the captain is going to receive a decoration, but he is also being investigated for indiscipline, they're about to send him back to Cuba for having woken up the entire battalion in the middle of the night and turning them into an army of shadows. We bring the three prisoners. We set the hut on fire with the two dead inside, and we take the mortar and the Uzis.

"These Uzis aren't worth shit," the company leader says, inspecting them. "They're only good for hand-to-hand combat."

The commander of my company, Lieutenant Amado Salvaterra, doesn't have the gift of leadership. He watches everything from behind thick bottle glasses that give his delicate features a perpetual look of surprise, so he relies heavily on his sergeants,

152

especially Carlos, who leads the company on the return to our permanent location, crushing the weeds with his feet in their Romanian boots. I keep my head down to keep from seeing the whirlwind of the dead sweep away the souls of the Savimbi guerrillas we killed. For now, they are at peace, for now. Next to me, Agustín marches with his PKM machine gun slung across his back. It's only nine in the morning, but the sun is already beating down strongly, almost hatefully, so I look up, the dead are fading, I can barely see them, but one of them, I can't tell who because of the hard light, says to me: "Cassandra."

It comes in a whisper, and I know my life is running out. The Erinyes are already beginning to chant again, *It's unraveling, it's unraveling.*

They chant for me, although they know I won't return to Cuba in one of those caskets that become nothing, I'll remain here in the red earth of Angola until a hyena digs up my bones and my skull goes on to the Cunene River and then the dust I will become goes on to the ocean and, finally, the marine currents take me to Hellespont, but not yet, for now. For now, I am very alive, sitting on the balcony of my house, watching the street. I'm not yet a little tin soldier, the whirlwind of the dead is not yet spinning over my head.

The captain. The captain looks at me and it's as if he doesn't see me. The captain looks at me but doesn't look at me. The captain looks at his beloved wife who lies in Cuba and looks like me. I am not inside the captain's eyes, she is, the one who no longer is.

"Tell your sergeant that you have to come to my tent tonight," he says, without looking at me.

"At your command, my captain," I say, my voice shrill, and salute.

I stand so firm that I look like a candle, but he doesn't say anything for a while. Then he says, "You have the same blue eyes as her."

It's just a whisper that comes out of his mouth on that cold Angolan morning, when the leopard no longer exists and my time is running out, Zeus who reigns on Olympus, but that murmur is my death sentence and I know it, I know it before the captain says in that sonorous voice, "Soldier, you may withdraw."

I know it as I hold the military salute, with my hand very close to my eyes, looking at the captain's very black eyes that contemplate my own but don't see me, I know it as we're surrounded by the clamor of the soldiers and officers playing baseball. I know it when I go to see Carlos and I tell him that the captain says to give me authorization to go to his tent at night. Carlos is next up to bat and needs to concentrate, he watches the ball go from the pitcher to the catcher and it's all the same to him where I spend the night, he barely lifts his olive-green-cap-covered head to say, "Go get fucked, Marilyn Monroe, do what the captain tells you. Whatever the captain commands. I'm sure it's so you can write one of those crazy long little letters of yours."

"Yes, probably," I tell him, because we're getting along, in a way. We were in two combat missions together, and he saw me advance with the rest.

I try to read. The pages of *Anna Karenina* unfold before my eyes, but I can't manage to focus. Lyudmila gave me that novel, one morning when we all went out in the old Chevy, she, my father, and I. We were singing a Silvio Rodríguez song along the way, our voices crossing, they were going in parallel and then, suddenly, they fused together on that cool September morning. Her voice and mine, because my father wasn't singing, my father was so focused on the steering wheel that he seemed to have melded into the car. The Russian woman was happy, her mother had arrived from Kiev and she was planning a half-Russian, half-Ukrainian meal for our return.

We're going in the Chevy to the university in the city of Santa Clara, Lyudmila was offered a job there, much better paid than in Cienfuegos, so she and my father are weighing the possibility of moving to that city in the center of the island.

We're going.

The idea of moving to Santa Clara, a landlocked city, makes my father nervous. But he's happy to know that he'll no longer see the Black professor who usually comes to visit the apartment. After drinking the tea the Russian woman serves alongside cookies purchased at the variety store, while Alla Pugacheva's voice comes from the Philips record player, singing in Spanish with a strong Slavic accent *casarse por amor . . . no pudo ser tratándose de un rey*, this professor remains seated on the sofa with Lyudmila, going over their curriculum. During these visits, my father cracks those mechanic's fingers of his that can tighten screws without need of a wrench, and looks at the professor with hatred.

We arrive at the university in Santa Clara. We park the Chevy and walk over to the Literature Department.

The dean traveled to Istanbul two weeks ago and won't be back for two months, but the department secretary shows us the classrooms and even the student dorms, and goes on and on about how the university was designed by a famous Japanese architect and how the library contains the third largest collection of books in Cuba. She lists a series of authors and titles that makes Lyudmila nod her head several times, then she looks closely at me and at the Russian woman for a long time and remarks that she's amazed by how much we resemble each other. She doesn't say anything about my father, perhaps she thinks he's the driver. My father is dressed in a plaid shirt, Jiquí-brand jeans, and a pair of Russian boots that are too big for him. It's hard for my father and for me to find shoes that fit our small feet. We could use children's shoes, but we don't. My father's nails aren't all that clean. It's not hard to notice the grease from all the cars.

"It's all very nice. You can even sense the knowledge in the wall hangings," the Russian woman says, watching the secretary's plump hands move restlessly as she rambles on.

"That's true, Lyudmila. Was your son born here or in Russia? How old is he? Thirteen?"

I look like a thirteen-year-old boy, I'm a kind of awkward Peter Pan who never grows up. My father doesn't exist to this woman, you can tell she's not used to dealing with poorly shaven men who don't wash their hands thoroughly and whose new clothing hangs on them as if it were borrowed.

"He was born here," Lyudmila says. She doesn't like having to elaborate on the details of her life. "And this is my husband."

When he hears "husband," my father stands up tall, as if the Russian woman just gave him a medal.

"Ah, look at that," the woman manages to utter, and then we go to the dean's office and the Russian woman signs a contract. For now she'll have to travel by taxi to Santa Clara every Friday to teach the students who look at us in surprise when we peek into their classrooms, as if they had never before seen a Russian woman, a tiny mechanic with the brawny arms of a much larger man, and a very thin teenager with the face of a girl.

Ten pesos is what Lyudmila's weekly round-trip taxi will cost, and this seems like a fortune to my father, but he doesn't say anything.

We get into the Chevy and go to the center of Santa Clara to have some soda and a beer in a bar with air conditioning and old music. *The door closed behind you,* I can hear Tejedor sing with a suave, plaintive voice from a record player that couldn't be more of an antique. My father seems somewhat melancholy and concerned: I'm leaving for Angola and he doesn't like Santa Clara. Lyudmila is excited, she puts her hand on my father's arm and looks at him with laughter in her eyes.

"Let's go to Vidal Park, they told me it's the prettiest thing in this city. But, please, do something about those funeral faces."

"Okay," my father says.

He calls over the waiter and pays the bill, grumbling a little, but not too much.

The park is full of trees and neoclassical buildings. The Russian woman sees a bookstore and it's like something lights up inside of her. She lets out an enthusiastic squeal and drags my father and me inside.

On the table of new releases is the first Cuban edition of *Anna Karenina,* translated by Eliseo Diego.

"How much is it?" Lyudmila asks.

"Three pesos," the bookseller says, his voice too singsongy for my father, who throws him a stern look.

Lyudmila buys the book and gives it to me, with a special dedication. *For Raulito, because I love him even more than my future children.* The Russian woman is thirty-five years old but looks younger; my father is fifty but looks older, so she and I can both pass for children of his. He's in a bad mood because the beer wasn't as cold as he expected.

"These piece-of-shit Santa Clarans, somehow they know I'm from Cienfuegos."

"Please shut up, you're not the center of the world," Lyudmila says.

"I say whatever I want," my father says and then falls into a silence from which we don't escape until we arrive in Cienfuegos and get out in front of the building where I live with my mother. Before I go upstairs, the Russian woman gives me a hug and a kiss and a "Take good care of yourself, Raulito, when you're over there," and my father gives my hand one of those squeezes that nearly grind my bones and says, "You know, my son . . ." and since he doesn't finish his sentence, I am left without knowing what I know.

From the first step on the stairs, I watch them get into the car, I hear the engine and I see the Russian woman's arm leaning on the open window with that gesture that is so like her, that makes her seem like a character out of a Hollywood movie.

"Svetlana gave you this crap," my mother says when she sees me arrive with the book.

"Her name isn't Svetlana," I say for the hundredth time, and my mother's eyes tear up.

"You're a traitor."

"I know, but what can you do? That's how things are. I like the Russian woman and she's kind to me. Would you want for her to be cruel?"

"I don't want anything," my mother says, and then she adds, "I want all of you to go and leave me alone, especially you, you goddammed fag."

My mother calls me a fag one September afternoon, when I've just returned from Santa Clara, she does so while looking me in the eye. I wait for what will follow, I wait for her to hug me and ask for forgiveness, like always. She has had too much to drink and you can tell. The whole house shines impeccably, she was always very clean, but over each piece of furniture and on the walls lies the unmistakable patina of sadness. On the wall facing the balcony is the large portrait from when she and Nancy turned fifteen, Nancy so blond and my mother so dark-haired, fixed in the smiles that divide both girls' faces in two.

N ow the captain is lying in the hammock, caressing the material of the synthetic silk dress he bought me in Luanda before he found out his wife had died in Gibara while he was making me dance like Olivia Newton-John.

I'm fifteen years old. I've given the Russian woman my poems. The ones I wrote in my chemistry notebook. She read them and then invited me to the Malecón, and there, alongside the sea, she looked at me with her eyes full of tears and hugged me tightly and we spent a long time like that, and then it started to rain, and she kept the notebook. I gave it to her so I wouldn't make any more trouble for myself, since the word *angel* appears in one of them, and when the chemistry teacher read that, they took me straight to the principal's office and the principal said, "Ideological diversionism."

"He's suffering from ideological diversionism," they tell my father. "Be careful, this could ruin the future of such an intelligent young man."

I don't have a future, I'm a tree with roots in the sand, I wish my father could know this, and my mother, who is now hanging the laundry on the balcony as she sings. She met someone, an engineer from Santiago who came to work in the new oil refinery, and she's happy. She's going out tonight, but things won't turn out as she'd hoped. The engineer, who studied in the German Democratic Republic and lived for a long time in Havana, will ask her to engage in sexual acts that my prudish mother won't be willing to perform, so it'll be ciao, end of relationship. My mother will come back home like a withered flower, and sit in the living room like a withered flower, and with a sole gesture of her hand, she will prevent me from speaking to her and then look at me with a sad smile.

"You won't get to meet Juan Carlos," my mother will say in barely more than a whisper.

"Juan Carlos?" I'll ask, playing dumb.

"Yes, that idiot. He wanted to stick his thing in my mouth," my mother will explain.

I go to my room and dress like a woman, I put on my makeup carefully, I kneel down before her and take her hands in mine and look into her eyes and then she smiles, and I am her sister, and we're both virginal and good.

We're both crazy.

"My good name depends on your silence," the captain says to me in a serious tone and it's as if he said, "I'm going to kill you and the bullets will cross your body and come out the other side and then they'll even blow through the *quimbos* where the women already have the fires lit, ready to mash the cassava until it becomes a hard, white, crunchy dough." Cassava that I won't taste because a part of soldier Raúl Iriarte's brain will be flying along, stuck to one of those bullets.

The rest of you, Olivia Newton-John, the captain thinks, will fall into the weeds as the bullets keep flying through Angola, and then he thinks that I look so much like her, the deceased, that I look so much like her that if I put on the dress, perhaps I will become the deceased, that's what he tells me.

"Put this on, soldier Raúl Iriarte, and put on some makeup."

He holds out the dress and the slender-heeled shoes and then turns his back to me and goes outside to watch the Angolan night as I curl my eyelashes with great care, apply very black mascara to them that the captain purchased at an exclusive shop in Luanda, not for me, but for the one who died in Holguín of methanol poisoning, then I use the blood-red lipstick and next to me is Aphrodite, it's the first time I've seen her since I became Raulito Iriarte, aka Spineless, aka Wendy, aka Marilyn Monroe, aka Olivia Newton-John.

Aphrodite is wearing the clothes of an Olympic goddess, and locks of long, curly hair fall over her forehead.

"You were never anything special, oh, Cassandra, daughter of Priam, you never stood out among the women of Ilios, there were always more beautiful ones than you, but to make up for that whole thing with Paris, Helen, and the apple, if you want, I can envelop you in a cloud, so that the captain can't see you while I take you out of the encampment and save your life."

I give her no reply, it's not worth it. She lies as much as Odysseus the false. After making myself up, I put on the silk dress and the high heels and, standing at the center of the tent under the kerosene lamp that illuminates me with a phantasmagoric, spectral light, I hope the captain turns around and sees me. When he turns toward me it's as if all the captains are turning in all the parallel and infinite worlds that he and I inhabit. In some of those worlds, we haven't gone to Angola, in others, we haven't survived the battle against the South Africans, in some, she is alive and I am dead, in others, she and I are dead and the captain is alive, and in still others, she and I are alive and it is the captain who is not there, and the strangest thing, father Zeus who knows everything, is that in some of these worlds, you don't exist, and neither does Olympus with all of its gods, neither was there an Ilios nor an Achilles who led the Myrmidons, nor an Odysseus who took his time in finding the way back to Ithaca, father Zeus. The captain has whipped around like the whirlwind of the dead whips over our heads and then he has called me by her name, the name of the dead woman who is rotting in the municipal cemetery over there in Holguín, beneath a tombstone with the epitaph: *Rest in peace, Katerina, you could have lived a long life, but fate had other plans for you.* The captain has again called me by her name and he has spent himself in an embrace that wears me out as well, the longest embrace in the world, while the bullets that will kill me still rest inside his automatic rifle. To kill me, he will have to tell me we're going somewhere and put his hand on my back and lead me to the bush so that I disappear and he can later say, "The hyenas took him away."

Or perhaps a leopard or a hungry lioness, perturbed by the sound of war, took him away, she pulled him out of the hammock and took him off to feed her hungry cubs, the captain will suggest, the captain who will have the decency to bury me in that deep hole I dug during a day of punishment. The captain will take me to the bush, and then he'll come back to the bush to confirm whether I'm really dead, to confirm whether he killed Raúl Iriarte or Katerina Rodríguez Morales, the captain will go to the bush, will shoo away the hyenas and the vultures with gunfire, and will return with what is left of me to the unit. That's how things will go, father Zeus, you who know everything. Or did I leave something out? The captain has turned to take a good look at me and he has embraced me and then he has said, "You look so much like her."

He has hardly murmured it, so close to my ear, and I've kneeled down and opened his fly, but his penis is dead.

"Stand up," he says.

"You're a whore," he says.

just want to sing like Roberto Carlos," my brother says.

"But you're not Roberto Carlos," my father emphasizes, his tone fraught with rancor. "If I find out that you missed school again, well, you'll see."

"But first, listen to me," my brother says.

"I don't have anything to listen to, it's all settled," my father says and I'm in my room reading *The Iliad* and I hear my brother's voice, strong but shot through with nerves.

"*El gato que está en nuestro cielo / No va a volver a casa si no estás . . .*"

"I told you not to sing," my father says, and then I hear the first blow, clear as the beating of a drum.

"What I say goes around here."

My mother isn't around.

"You go to hell," my brother says. "You're not going to lay a hand on me again."

I peek out of the door of my room and I see them, motionless as wax statues, one with his arm raised up high, the other covering his face. You have stopped time so that I can again see them like that, you in your infinite mercy have given me the possibility of seeing in my father's blue eyes, in my brother's yellow ones, the reflection of the bronze swords of Ilios. I've seen my father's eyes and I've remembered my brother Hector, not fleeing before Achilles the terrible, but rather the Hector from before the war of Ilios began, and I've realized that we humans are no more than avatars, shadows that you send to the earth to entertain yourself, why do you do it? You should know, omnipotent father Zeus. Who is Cassandra to interrogate you? I am no one, I've gotten lost in the dark depths of time, I've gone along opening the doors to rooms with transparent glass walls and in one of them, I found my red and insatiable heart as it beats. I contemplated it as if it were not mine and then a bunch of anxious tourists came up behind me to photograph it with their cheap cameras and I felt the leopard, who no longer exists, brushing up against my back. I felt him, the leopard has crossed imaginary eras and approached me, father Zeus, to tell me, it has approached me amid the beating echoes of the Angolan women preparing the cassava we will no longer eat, because we all have died, father Zeus, all.

"My good name depends on your silence," the captain repeats and he pushes me with both hands and tells me to sit down and he holds out the letter that is already old, yellowed, and crumpled.

"Read it," he orders and then opens a bottle of whiskey and pours some of the golden liquid into the lids of the two canteens.

I sit in one of the canvas chairs and he sits in the other and watches me as I read, but this time he doesn't cry and it's as if it doesn't hurt him. He still has his fly undone and the gland of his withered penis sticks out. He orders me to lie down in the hammock and pull down my panties. I'm on my belly, with my mouth resting on the pillow. I guess that the captain is unbuckling his belt and I hear him tell me, "Don't yell or it will be worse."

He beats me, I drown my screams, and with each blow, his penis gets stiffer. Then he sinks into me like someone who's reached the shore.

"Fucking faggot," he whispers into my ear as he moves.

I receive a letter from my brother just as I am about to leave for Angola:

When I lived in Cuba, I was crazy. In Cuba, there's no life, just Fidel Castro's speeches and police who want to shave your head if they think you're getting too shaggy. It was too much for me, I had to leave. But I'm fine, don't worry. And don't go to Angola, don't pay attention to those degenerates, don't pay attention to that shithead dad of ours. Wait for me to claim you or send you a speedboat to take you to Key West and then you can make your life. I know you dress as a woman, but I don't care. Everyone makes their own ship out of their lives and enters whichever ocean they want. I'm singing here, I bought myself an old mobile home and I'm going around Florida and they give me free food. I had to leave the Black girl, I couldn't deal with her missing an eye, it made me so fucking sad, but that's how things are, Raulito, frustrating. Tell our old lady I'm fine, and send Papá to fucking hell for me. The States isn't what I expected, but you can live here and you don't have the 6 p.m. speech drilling a hole in your head, or those snitches from the Committee for the Defense of the Revolution asking around about you all the time. So I'm happy, and I don't have any problems with anyone. I don't go around beating up on anyone, and now I have an American girlfriend, a big Black girl who's almost twice my size, but she's one of those women they don't make anymore. Don't go to Angola, there's nothing for you there. That's the craziest thing I've heard: Raulito Iriarte in Angola. What kind of warrior are you? Is the Russian woman still with Papá? That Russian woman is crazy, but Papá is crazier than she is. That Russian woman is too good for Papá, and Papá isn't the kind to be a cuckold. So there will be blood, I'm telling you, Raulito, you'll see.

F ucking faggot," the captain says to me as he moves on top of me and puts his fingers in my mouth, and outside, the dog that someone brought from Luanda barks. He's the unit's pet.

I am the captain's pet.

"No one is born a soldier," he suddenly says to me. "But no one dies a soldier, either."

He says this thinking of her, the dead woman, the one who breathed her last in Cuba, where it's not as easy to die as it is in Angola. Then he keeps talking to me.

"I was among the first, among the ones who stopped the Afrikaners when they came to take over Bengala. I remember that Agostinho Neto proclaimed the independence of Angola so that the last Portuguese troops would allow our planes to land at the airport in Luanda. In other words, my combat record is very long. That's why you need to be very careful about what you say, you understand, Olivia?"

He calls me Olivia as he moves on top of me. It hurts, but I've learned to bear it. When he is done, he slaps my ass hard and orders me to put on my military uniform and go back to my quarters. He doesn't want me next to him.

"I can't stand you. I know you knew she had died, but you didn't say anything, out of jealousy and cruelty. You're cruel, Olivia Newton-John."

"How could I know it?"

"Don't pretend, I know you're a witch. I've seen your eyes change color when something's going to happen, I've seen them go from blue to an intense black, strange . . . what's the word? Treacherous. Go back to the other soldiers and watch what you say. If I hear that there's even the slightest rumor about what happens in this tent, if someone looks at me with even the slightest hint of mockery and then looks at you, I'll kill you, Raúl Iriarte, don't doubt that I'll kill you," the captain says, and then he turns his back to me.

I leave.

Johnny the Rocker will receive a medal for having killed that guerrilla who was sleeping in the hut like a princess under a spell. The guerrilla, recruited for the price of a little bit of food for him and for his family in Cabinda, still doesn't realize he's dead, so he wanders the battalion, looking at us Cubans with eyes wide with amazement. Sergeant Carlos and I perceive him. But Carlos doesn't know who he is, he only feels his presence, he can't see him clearly.

"We've got to do a spiritual cleanse here," he says. "There are strange, bad presences around, and they hate us."

I do see the Angolan, sitting on the grass, close to the mess hall. He watches with ancestral hunger as we take spoons full of rice, peas, and Spam to our mouths. He's a prisoner of the void of our encampment. He doesn't join the whirlwind of dead souls that spires over our heads. He follows Johnny the Rocker everywhere and wants to tell him about his young daughter who was left alone in Cabinda, he wants to tell him about when they put the rifle in his hands and explained what he had to press so that the bullets would come out to cut lives short.

Nós apreciamos a som das balas, são legal e perigoso como o trovão do dia chuvoso, the Angolan says in the Portuguese of an animated film character, but Johnny the Rocker doesn't hear him. He goes back and forth, whistling his usual rock and roll tunes, happier than a sunny Sunday. I do hear the Angolan and Athena translates everything he says for me. She's like that, she likes to torment me. Vainglorious, she appears astride a carriage of black, coarse-maned horses, she removes her helmet and looks at me with those owl eyes that are also my mother's eyes.

"No one is born a soldier," she says to me, "but no one dies a soldier, either."

Your daughter is really something, father Zeus. You can tell that she came out of your head dancing like a warrior. I taught her to play chess and after the second lesson, if I'd asked her to, she could have easily defeated Anatoly Karpov, Garry Kasparov, and Bobby Fischer.

"Intelligence is a matter for the goddesses," she used to say to me, looking at me with a placid smile.

I'm still a little tin soldier, with feet so small that I can't find boots to wear, they're all big on me, so I find myself forced to fill them in with a little bit of cotton the administration gives me. Even so, my feet get banged up, they're covered in blisters and Sergeant Carlos sends me to the infirmary.

"I don' wan' ya ta come back unti' ya foot shines all healthy," he says to me, garbling his words.

The newspapers *Granma* and *Juventud Rebelde* arrive at the unit, publicizing our feats. Never before were so many beaten by so few, the *Granma*'s editorial proclaims in large black letters. I read it in the infirmary. The article mentions our battalion and mentions the captain, and beneath the words is a photo in which we look thin and withered like flowers forgotten in a vase. We're all wearing helmets, but the captain, like the officer that he is, is also sporting his large, black mustache. He still doesn't know that she has died, so he looks proud of himself as he grips the strap of his rifle. Behind him are Carlos, Agustín, Osmel, the driver of the armored personnel carrier, killed by a Chinese-made shell, and me, looking like a girl who has been forced to put on that Soviet-made helmet that's too big for her.

The echoes of the Erinyes reach me, chanting still: *It's unraveling, it's unraveling, it's unraveling.*

I know that this time, they are singing for me.

"*Ay*, Cassandra," the Erinyes say. "This time no one can free you, you sully the glory of the glorious captain and, with it, that of the whole battalion, and with that of the battalion, that of the entire Cuban army."

———————

Y our feet are a mess," the nurse says to me, looking at me with a hint of compassion.

Then he smiles, goes to the medicine cabinet, and takes out a tube of analgesic cream and a bottle of Mercurochrome.

"Put these on after taking a shower," he says, and then puts his right hand on my knee and looks into my eyes. "Poor guy."

I sigh, I put on my socks and boots. Back in my company section, with each step I feel like I can't take another one. I never imagined that dying would be such an arduous matter.

I need the captain to make up his mind.

Saturdays and Sundays are the worst days in the unit. The hours drag like a leopard in agony, and once the soldiers get bored of baseball, soccer, basketball, and the music of Silvio Rodríguez and Pablo Milanés, they look for someone to mock. Now, without the captain's protection, I'm the best option.

"Come here, Marilyn Monroe, sing something for us," Sergeant Carlos says, and when he doesn't see me, because I'm usually lying in the hammock reading, he goes to the tent and shouts an order at me to come out, to not be such a faggot. I leave the book on the hammock, I put on my boots and go out. The captain is in his tent. I know he can hear them shouting "Marilyn Monroe" at me, that they're forcing me to grip the bat so I can learn to play baseball, a manly man's sport, a real Cuban man's, not one for little girls who look British, or worse, South African.

"Look straight ahead," Carlos orders. "If the ball hits you because you're fucking around, that won't be my fault."

Then he moves about sixty feet from me, climbs onto the small mound of flattened dirt, and imitates the warm-up movements of big league pitchers. The only ones playing are Johnny the Rocker, in the role of catcher, Carlos, and me. The other soldiers watch us, not with pride, but in a trance. I have the bat in hand. The ball in Carlos's hands is hard, a Batos ball that the captain brought from Cuba. It's so dirty it looks like it could never have been white. I raise the bat and look into Carlos's eyes. He's going to use the arm he has trained for hours and hours in the unit's improvised gym to hurl the ball at my head. I know it. Athena whispers it in my ear.

"Duck down in time, because it's not your day yet," the goddess demands of me, and when the ball leaves Carlos's hand, I drop the bat and fall to the ground. The ball ends up in the hands of Johnny the Rocker, who shouts in a feigned American accent, "Estreye one!"

"What do you mean, strike? He almost split his head open," says Agustín, who's sitting on the grass alongside the other soldiers.

"I caught it here," Johnny the Rocker says, standing up and indicating his chest. "It was a curveball up the middle. Carlos here was born for baseball."

"I'm a cousin of Braudilio Vinent," Carlos says, and then, in a voice that is simultaneously exhausted, harsh, and soft: "Get ready, Marilyn, here it comes."

He pitches at me again, and again I throw myself to the ground.

"Is this baseball or rhythmic gymnastics?" Carlos shouts. He threatens, "If you duck again, Marilyn, I'm going to assign you a punishment detail, that's an order! Are you a man or a cockroach? Grab the bat, dammit!"

He forgot to add the "Monroe." I grab the bat and look at Carlos's dark eyes. Carlos is the New Man, born to shine in these times, my Zeus, everything he does is for the benefit of the fatherland, he calls me Marilyn Monroe for the benefit of the fatherland, he forces me to play baseball for the benefit of the fatherland, which is so far away, over there in the Caribbean. I'm playing baseball on a sunny day in Angola. We're playing baseball so the rest of the battalion can watch us and laugh, everyone except the officers who are focused on other matters. We play baseball and *Anna Karenina* has been left open on my hammock and I think someone could steal it from me to wipe his ass and then I'd be even more alone, even more abandoned than ever, alone with the gods, alone with Apollo, who, standing behind Carlos, anoints the sergeant's arm so that the ball flies straight at my head. The god's curly locks move like thin serpents behind Carlos.

Agustín gets up from his spot on the grass.

"That's enough," he roars. "I'm going to bat. Give me the bat, Marilyn Monroe."

He calls me Marilyn Monroe without realizing it, but those words open up an abyss, and I'm on one side while he's on another. Marilyn Monroe he calls me, and Marilyn Monroe I'll remain, and although he's trying to help me, it's as if he's wiped away that afternoon we spent with the Russian woman, my father, and my mother, when they came to visit me, just before we left for Angola, and my father put his hand on his shoulder and looked him in the eye and told him we should take care of one another and respect each other. My father, that tiny man with his brawny, circus-freak arms, asked another man a favor, asked him to please defend his son, asked, perhaps for the first time, and the Russian woman took the teenager's hand and added, "Please, Agustín, you can see how shy and withdrawn he is."

But there's no one who can defend me, it's too risky to defend me, so when Agustín gets up to bat for me and calls me Marilyn Monroe like the others, I know I am lost, an aimless breeze. Only the gods accompany me. Athena, Apollo, Ares, and Aphrodite sit next to me on the grass and watch Agustín get ready to bat.

In the other photo of our battalion that ran in the *Juventud Rebelde* newspaper, I don't appear, and neither does the captain. Carlos, Agustín, Johnny the Rocker, and Lieutenant Amado Salvaterra sit on top of a shiny T-55M tank, looking at the camera with defiance. They don't look like the little tin soldiers that they are. In that photo, we're "the Cubans." UNITA soldiers run away when they sense that we're nearby; we need only dress the FAPLA in Cuban uniforms to make our foes scatter. I go back to the infirmary and sit down on the cot with my feet up in the air and I read this newspaper. The nurse looks at me with compassion and lets me stay a while longer. He's forty-two years old and has a degree in nursing.

"I like reading and French movies," he tells me, "and I see how badly the other soldiers treat you, and I don't like the abuse or the fucking around, because I'm not like the rest of them . . ."

"That's good."

"What's good?"

"That you're not like the rest of them."

"Ah. You have such nice skin," he says, just like the captain would whisper in my ear.

I nod. He waits for me to elaborate, to tell him my troubles or my deepest secrets. I don't say anything and then the nurse takes his right hand to my face and caresses my cheeks.

"He's not going to find out," he says, and I know who he is talking about, and I know what the nurse is trying to do, now that we're in the infirmary alone, because it's Sunday and most people are out playing baseball while the rest are writing letters to their families, letters that begin with the lines, the indispensable lines, *I hope this finds you well today, I'm doing well.* I say nothing and the nurse suddenly gets very serious and takes a distant attitude of civil professionalism and military virility.

"Everything is fine with that foot, soldier Raúl Iriarte, you can rejoin the company."

He's not going to find out, he just said to me, his voice syrupy. They're talking about us. The battalion is one enormous ear that listens to everything we say, then turns around and talks about it. They're talking about us, the captain and I are connected by an invisible thread that he can't untie anymore, even if he stops seeing me, even if he feigns indifference. They're talking about us and we're under suspicion, he'll never again be able to stand on the platform to rally the battalion without eyes going from him to me, and all of his gestures, no matter how virile and warrior-like, will forever be nothing but a simulacrum behind which he's trying to hide. The captain is no longer a hero, even though he was in the papers. The captain is silence and a concealed gesture. The division's unspeakable military police are going to investigate him and the same dark officer who told him about his wife's death in Cuba will come to tell him that they're after him because of a suspicion so terrible that he doesn't dare put it into words, a suspicion that links him to a certain soldier named Raúl Iriarte. The captain will not stand upon hearing this, he will pretend that he can't believe it, his mustache will stop looking so smug, he will bang loudly on the table and spit out, "How dare you?"

"It's just an investigation," the dark officer will say. "You know how gossip is. We received an anonymous tip."

"Who sent it?"

"It's anonymous. How should I know?" the dark lieutenant says, and smiles.

"My good name depends on your silence," you said to me, Captain, and I kept my silence, but your good name is on everyone's tongues, and although you push me away and don't want to have anything to do with me, although I am nothing but an aimless breeze to you, you and I are tied together by the invisible thread that brings us ever closer together, fusing us into one.

I can hear the *tam tam* of the Angolan women beating the wood in unison and that *tam tam* reveals us and the captain can't look into the dark lieutenant's eyes and say, "It's just that he looked so much like her."

He can't say anything. He knows that any gesture of agreement will permanently distance him from that lieutenant with such dark skin, who is also from Holguín and who can't conceive of the captain choosing any course of action but shooting himself in the temple and leaving a letter that says that he has been hounded by rumors and is dying to preserve his honor as a respectable revolutionary soldier. But the captain isn't thinking of suicide, he knows he will return to Holguín to contemplate the place where his wife rests forever.

"When they came to me with the rumor, I told them no, that I knew you from cadet school, that you were always a real man, and that here, if there's anything in abundance, it's women, that you had no need . . . Was I right?" the lieutenant asks and looks pleadingly at the captain, he needs the reply to be yes, that he was right. He needs it like the thirsty, wounded leopard needed water, but the captain doesn't reply, he gets up from his folding chair and leaves the tent and sniffs at the night air again, but today he won't be allowed, he won't be allowed to go out hunting for UNITA guerrillas. He's obliged to reply. The words dog him and close in on him, the words besiege him.

"Was I right?" resounds in the air, a murmur that won't fade away, like the flame of a candle, sometimes bright, sometimes flickering, never fully going out.

I am lying in the hammock and the captain can feel me, it's as if I were walking on his body. I, Cassandra, walk on the captain's body like an aimless breeze and he feels it. He feels me, and I am guilty of coming to Angola to ruin his life. That is why Rauli must die, the captain thinks, and he needs to use my nickname to imagine me lost in the night.

M arilyn Monroe, Agustín called me, just like that, without
thinking about it, without meaning to offend me, he called
me Marilyn Monroe like someone calls a tree a tree and a rock a
rock. *Marilyn Monroe you called me, so Marilyn Monroe I'll stay.
Now go ask your mother what she and I do when we play,* I could
say in response, but it would be a bad joke. Agustín's mother is
dead, killed due to a failure of one of those kerosene and alcohol
stoves that take your head off when they explode. Agustín was
adopted by an aunt named Zoila Cornejo, who worked as the
concierge of the elementary school we both attended, and whom
students and teachers nicknamed *Soy la Conejo,* "I am the rab-
bit." Agustín stood up for his aunt and sang old boleros at school
concerts. He would sing after some fourth-grade girl who swung
her arms left and right, almost like the blades of a windmill, and
recited that thing about how *the mountains cried when they killed
Che,* then it would be Agustín's turn to perform one of those
boleros composed by Comandante Juan Almeida, about whom
we only knew that he appeared in photos in the history books,
raising his arm behind Fidel Castro in a *dril cien* linen suit and a
clean-shaven face. Agustín would sing that bolero about a pretty

Mexican woman, kind and courteous, and we would applaud, and the teachers would say he was very masculine, nearly a heartthrob, and that he'd have a future in sports. But then he was just two points shy of getting into the Upper School for Advanced Athletics and the army recruited him, like it did me.

"The olive-green monster got you," Agustín's father said when he came to say goodbye as we were about to leave for Angola.

Agustín's father, Black, tall, a truck driver, with a thick, gold chain at his neck, his hand on Zoila Cornejo's shoulder, smiles as if there were something to be happy about. We're leaving for Angola and the Russian woman and my parents still haven't arrived, so Agustín's father removes a box of Populares cigarettes from the pocket of his Western-made jeans and offers them to us and the four of us smoke, standing, close to the garden of the unit called Loma Blanca, a place for deployment, before leaving for Angola.

"Behave yourselves over there," says the father, who looks a lot like his son.

Zoila Cornejo has long hands and sharp eyes behind black-rimmed glasses. She's very thin; she didn't have children and she's already too old to have them. There was always a complicity between her and Agustín that's noticeable in small gestures, just signals, like fixing his shirt collar and softly squeezing his hand. She hasn't said anything since she arrived. You can tell that it has been very hard for her to see her surrogate son with a buzz cut and dressed as a soldier, ready to depart. My mother hasn't arrived. I take two people from my mother with me when I leave, her sister Nancy and her son Raúl. They'll all arrive nearly at the same time, my father, the Russian woman, and her. My mother in a taxi and the other two in that old Chevy my father is so proud of.

"Hey, everyone," my father will say by way of greeting, and he'll squeeze Agustín's father's hand tightly to demonstrate who the real man is.

Agustín's father will eye the Russian woman in appreciation, a barely veiled look, and the Russian woman will look at him with a wide smile. After she arrived in Cuba and before she met my father, every husband, boyfriend, and lover the Russian woman had was Black, very dark-skinned, like Agustín's father, and my father knows it, so he puts his arm around Lyudmila's shoulders and tightens his belt.

"Let's sit down," he says, in a voice that is hoarser than usual.

My father has barely spoken to me, he has to play his manly man role and I am just a teenager without any muscles or facial hair, practically the photo negative of everything he is. The Russian woman has given me a kiss and my mother hugged me tightly and wet my cheeks with her tears, then she started to talk to Zoila Cornejo, and we all went to sit down by the trees among the other relatives of soldiers leaving for Angola.

"We'll be gone before we know it," Agustín says, kicking at the dirt with his right foot. "I hope we end up in the same unit."

"Yeah," I say, although I know that one day he'll call me Marilyn Monroe, just like that, without thinking about it, as if it were the most natural thing in the world, I know that one day he'll take my place in the game.

"That's enough, I'm going to bat. Give me the bat, Marilyn Monroe."

He takes the wooden bat from me, convinced along with the others that I'm incapable of hitting the ball, and pity will drive us apart, will make us strangers to each other forever. *A stranger, you'll be a stranger.* I think of those verses by a Cienfuegos poet as I watch Agustín take his place at home plate and look fiercely at Carlos, who laughs.

"Some girls have all the luck with boyfriends!"

"Enough with the jokes. Pitch, and send it down the center if you have the balls," Agustín says, drawing back the bat.

"Mine are big enough for your little girlfriend and you both!"

Carlos throws the ball. Agustín moves the bat at the right time. A powerful *toc* rings, deep and dry, and I see the ball fly away, it goes toward the weeds, it falls where the leopard once hid.

They hang the leopard's teeth around the necks of several soldiers. The captain wears two fangs from the upper jaw. I saw them when he undressed me and pushed me by the shoulders to kneel and kiss his penis. That image is indelibly engraved in the captain's memory as he continues to look out at the night, and still does not answer the question posed by the dark-skinned lieutenant.

"Was I right?" the lieutenant repeats, and also steps outside of the tent.

The African moon illuminates them both and they are gods beneath the whirlwind of the dead that awaits the reply, the entire Cuban army awaits the reply, and the animals in the thicket and the women who suspend the sound of the *tam tam* and the old men who stop telling their stories about princesses who rebel against the white man's power, they all await the reply, I await the reply. Lying in my hammock, with my cheek propped up on the pillow and my hands between my thighs as if to warm them up. Cassandra awaits the reply, my Zeus, she waits for the captain to come unfixed and for the world to keep turning, but the captain still does not reply and the universe holds its breath in vain and I'm seventeen years old and I'm dressed up as a woman and a boxer kisses me in the dark of a Cienfuegos club, thinking I'm very demure, very prudish and virginal, because I won't let his Black hand go down to my pelvis and touch my vagina, and I talk to him about the Beatles to distract him and to distract myself, because I am not feeling anything. I thought I was going to like it, I thought that when I kissed this man, as beautiful as the Ephebe of Marathon by Praxiteles, that desire was going to beat within me and rush through me, and what I have done until this moment and what I will do after is all for this, but no, I'm cold beneath the young man's kisses that seek my tongue and find it, and then he says that my hands are soft and that I'm the most beautiful woman he's ever seen, not just in Cuba, but out there, too, over in Texas where he went to compete. He says this as he gazes at me with his brown eyes, while Roberto Carlos sings *comenzó esta música suave . . .* , *qué bien si esta música suave no terminara jamás*, but it's going to end, Zeus who reigns on Olympus, that soft music will end, and with it, all music, and I'll be dressed as a woman in the middle of the club, and everyone will watch how I walk, how I move, how I swing my hips from side to side, lightly, almost not at all, *my soul falls in love / it falls in love / every time you come around my street.* They watch me move as I moved in Ilios when, in the company of the slaves, I crossed the agora and the Phoenician sailors pulled at their long black beards as I passed.

In three days, when we're in formation for breakfast, Johnny the Rocker will whisper that he needs to speak to me, but that what he has to tell me is such a big secret that no one can find out.

"Even if they torture you, you can't reveal what I tell you, Raúl."

I nod, and while we drink our *café con leche*, he begins by confessing that he heard it by accident, but now that he knows, he can't help but tell me, so I'm ready.

"They're saying things about the captain and you," Johnny says. "Be careful. Anyone can let off a stray shot, and then they'll say it was a UNITA attack, and you get rid of the rabies when you kill the dog, you get it?"

"Not really, but thanks, Johnny."

"You're welcome. I like you, Raúl, although I always thought this wasn't the right place for you, but it isn't the right place for any of us, and I've killed a man, I dug my bayonet into him and felt how that bayonet became part of him, it was like an organ vibrating in my hands, the strangest thing in the world. If I hadn't gone out to vomit, I would have gone crazy, and now I have a dead man on my conscience, you know? It's hard."

"What are you two whispering about?" Carlos says from one of the neighboring tables. "Hurry, we have to start."

Carlos also knows, you can tell by the way he looks at me, actually, Carlos always knew, Carlos also senses the dead, but not the gods, for him, the dead are a fog, a dreaminess, a pause when he stares out blankly. Carlos knows that I know too much, like the captain, who always knew that I knew his wife had died before the letter arrived, and who also knew that I could have warned Martínez that on a certain night one of Savimbi's little soldiers was going to fire an 82 mm projectile mortar at him and split him in two, and there would be no more Martínez or any more memories of the beautiful streets of the exclusive neighborhood of Miramar, or any more trips to the villages to look for *mulata* prostitutes, there wasn't going to be any more of that, Martínez would join the whirlwind of the dead that has followed us like a swarm of mosquitos ever since we arrived.

Martínez and the leopard's eyes.

"You're strange, Marilyn Monroe," Carlos says to me, but we're both strange, he and I, it's just that I'm stranger than he is, I am Cassandra and could speak to him of my time in Ilios, I could tell him that I was already here, before, in the Old World, but what does Carlos know of that? When I'm dead, on an August afternoon, my parents will sit down in the living room of what was once my house and will think about how everything began and they will blame *The Iliad*, a book so inappropriate for a hypersensitive boy, but then she'll say no, she'll say it all began when my father took me to the art gallery at Cienfuegos's Martí Park, where I saw Hieronymus Bosch's *Garden of Earthly Delights*, that I was never the same after, my mother will recall that I returned home nearly in tears, as if I'd found something in that triptych that terrified me, something that was too much for me, of an exaggerated too-muchness, without limits or containment.

"Something in him broke after seeing that painting," my mother will say, "and *The Iliad* only unleashed impulses that were already there."

Since the Russian woman is very far away, working in Santa Clara, my mother will dare show my father her intellectual superiority, she will treat him as what he is, a simple mechanic who never finished high school.

"I don't know how you caught my eye. I have never liked short men, but you tricked me, you were the only white man who knew how to dance like a Black one. I wanted to improve my genes, but not to marry some Spaniard with two left feet."

"You're the blabbermouth you always were. It's like a rain of flowers when you open your mouth, and not a soul can shut you up. Please, a little bit of peace, since we've already lost a son."

"I lost a sister too," my mother will say, trying to remember the real Nancy, but she'll only see me, with the dress she used to help me put on and the hairstyle I used to wear so that I could be her beloved sister for a while.

"But that was a long time ago already, and a sister isn't the same as a son."

"I know, don't remind me. If only we could bury Raulito properly and take him flowers, but he stayed over there in Angola."

"Maybe he's alive. No one saw the body, and you can't believe a single word out of these people. Maybe he's alive and well, reading those books of his, over in Zambia or Rhodesia, who knows."

"No, he died, I can feel it here, right in my chest, ever since the letter arrived, I have a tightness there that won't go away. Don't give me any hope, please, have a little mercy."

"Yes, it's better to think of him as dead."

They will have that conversation six months after I've died, but for now, I'm alive and I have to pretend that no one knows anything, even as I sense how they look at us. I'm standing in formation, behind Carlos, the sergeant, and in front of Matías, and listening to the captain, who is surrounded by the top brass and looks at us fiercely while he says we're sons of bitches, traitors, and that the rumormongers will pay dearly, that he who toys with a man's good name deserves to be thrown to the sea with a stone around his neck. All of them, officers, sergeants, and soldiers, remain silent, standing at attention, and the captain doesn't specify, but everyone knows he's referring to himself and to me. The captain's eyes travel over the battalion, taking in each one of the soldiers and officers, they stop at the bearers of the RPG rockets, the bearers of RPK machine guns, at the riflemen and their AKs, but they don't stop at me, it's as if I were invisible. The captain doesn't see me, his gaze glosses over the place where I am standing.

I am a shadow to him.

"The defamers will pay for this. To defame an officer of the Revolutionary Armed Forces without proof is a counterrevolutionary act that is severely punished. However . . . if the person who anonymously wrote to command, whether he be an officer, a sergeant, or a mere soldier, steps forward immediately and repents, now, in front of his colleagues, or explains the reasons for his behavior, we don't need to let this go any further, and everything can be excused."

No one says anything, the battalion now seems to be composed of shadows like me, because when he says this, the captain doesn't look at us, he now looks at some place above our heads.

"I'm waiting," the captain insists.

The dark-skinned lieutenant is also there, waiting. The unanswered question "Was I right?" also whirs above our heads. He returned to the regiment's brass without an answer. He will tell the colonel that the captain was so shaken by this attack to his name that he was speechless.

"He's really out of sorts." He'll say this and then settle into the sofa without the colonel's leave to do so. He's nothing more than an envoy of the High Command, like Prince Andrew in *War and Peace*, but his powers transcend his rank as first lieutenant, he's with State Security and is destined to be Fidel Castro's personal guard and go to Havana and live in Punto Cero, where he'll eat like a king. He can't vouch for the captain even though they've known each other for a long time, the captain has been accused of sodomy, and that cannot be permitted. By allowing the slightest suspicion to arise, he has already crossed the line. The dark-skinned lieutenant can't do anything for him.

They're going to interrogate us, the captain knows it, and he can't trust me, and more than that, he's sure that I'm going to break, that I'll tell everything, with tears in my eyes. Besides, the captain thinks as he stands before our formation without looking at anyone in particular, when the military prosecutors see how effeminate he is, this whore, we'll both be sentenced on the spot, unless . . . the captain keeps thinking, unless Olivia Newton-John dies, if bullets take her to a place from which there is no return, after all, it will be no great loss, she doesn't seem destined to live very long. Then there would be no one to interrogate and everything would be clean, clear, and simple, like the bird's wings that are Cuba and Puerto Rico.

Puerto Rico, wing that fell down to the sea,
unable to fly,
come fly with me
and we'll go in search of the same sky.

Pablo Milanés can be heard over the encampment's loudspeakers on a Sunday when Agustín and I are sitting together, playing chess, which we haven't done for a long time.

Even Agustín avoids looking at me, he concentrates on the pieces, moves his queen, picks her up and places her down on the board again. I could invoke the FIDE rule that states that once you touch a piece, you've played it, but I don't. No one calls me Marilyn Monroe anymore, there's something in the air that prevents them from calling me that, and it's that everyone knows: the captain is going to kill me. You can tell that he's not going to let it happen, he's not going to let everything be ripped away from him so easily, and this is the only solution, so there's nothing to be done about it. They look at me like you look at a dead man, and they respect me. Even Carlos calls me soldier Raúl Iriarte, the few times he feels obliged to say something to me.

"I don't know what advice to give you," Agustín suddenly says. "If you told me, it would be easier. I can understand a lot of things."

I remember the Omara Portuondo song: *If I told you how I suffer / if you knew about the great sorrow I carry within me.*

"I don't have anything to tell you. Tell my father everything's fine, that I did it, go to my house and tell him, just him, and maybe he'll understand, but don't say anything to my mother or the Russian woman."

"What are you talking about?"

"You know."

And the young boxer knew that night he was kissing me, lit up by the club's strobe lights, he suspected it but didn't say anything. After kissing on the dance floor, we went out to the street and sat down. He offered me a cigarette and asked if I wanted to go to a hotel with him, to keep the party going.

"If you want, Wendy, Captain Hook can come, too, I have that friend for her, the one who does karate."

"I'd really like that, but I'm leaving tomorrow."

"To where? Havana? Or farther away? Are you leaving the country? Are you emigrating? Aren't you scared of airplanes? I'm very scared of them. Sometimes I dream that I'm looking through the window and I see the wing come off and I want to tell the pilot, but I can't talk. It's so weird, Wendy. I dream that and then I tell my girlfriend that the airplane was falling and she asks me if I was inside it or outside. To keep from scaring her, I tell her I was sitting on the seawall in Havana when I saw it fall into the waves."

"Ah, so you have a girlfriend?"

"What does that have to do with anything? Do you want to marry me? Because if so, let's go to the courthouse right now."

"I'm too young," I said and stood up. "I'm going to look for my friend."

"Fine, go off with that ugly girl, who looks like a man, by the way. Keep living your shitty life in Cienfuegos, asshole of the world. I wanted to take you to Havana."

"There's nothing I need in Havana. I told you, I'm leaving."

And it was true, I was leaving for Angola.

You see them appear on the horizon, first one, then many, and you'd like to mistake them for seagulls, but then the wings become wooden, helmets, oars, and what you took for the shrill bird's cry turns out to be an unmistakable human voice, these are the Achaeans disembarking, they haven't yet come to kill us, they want something, they want Helen. A sentinel in a short tunic and leather sandals enters the palace where I am with my father and only shouts, "Achaeans!"

We go to the walls. My father and all of his children. Except for Paris, who is still sleeping, and no one goes to wake him. I know they've come for her, for the witch.

"Let them take her," I tell my father.

Old Priam strokes his long beard and looks at his daughter, who, standing before him, looks even smaller than usual. He looks at the Achaean warriors who have already passed the altar consecrated to Poseidon, so close to the shore, and are advancing along the path leading to Ilios. There are just twenty of them. Priam could order their massacre if he wished, they're coming to ask for a king's condescension, they bring oil, myrrh, and a white horse with a dizzying mane. Odysseus is walking at the front of

193

them all; Priam recognizes him by his broad back and his way of avoiding eye contact. The rest march dismally, reserved, far from their usual games and chatter. It's a very sunny day and yet there's something sad in the air and the white-haired steed seems to intuit that it will be sacrificed to the god who bears the trident. They reach the wall. The archers prepare their deadly weapons and look at the king.

"Give her to them," whispers the dark-haired Cassandra.

The sun shines on their bare backs. Odysseus's spear clangs when he drops it in the dust and he says he comes in peace.

"Open the walls!" says the king, and my brother Hector looks at him, assuaged, naïve, he thinks everything can be settled with a footrace and a few amphoras of wine. My poor brother is the first to go out and embrace the somber Odysseus, who arrives in the name of the Atreides. I see eleven seagulls fly over the ten Achaean ships, one of the birds shrieks and dives into the sea in search of prey, then it's ten seagulls and ten ships. We have seen ten years of war, and in the eleventh year, Ilios will fall. I know it, it's branded with iron on the back of time and there's nothing to be done about it anymore, the votive offers to all the gods are in vain, the massacre is in vain, it is branded as if with fire, Ilios will fall and I look at my father with tears in my eyes.

M y brother José is waiting for me in the living room at home. They told him that I came home very late at night in a pair of shorts that barely covered my ass, that from behind I looked more like a woman than a man, the neighbor on the third floor told him, the one who loves Carlos Puebla and *tu querida presencia, / commandante Che Guevara*. It's practically the only song she listens to.

I'm seventeen years old, my brother doesn't live with us anymore, he's about to emigrate, but nonetheless, he's come to ask me to explain myself. He looks like me but with dark hair, a little bit taller, but not by much. He inherited my father's muscles. Under his tight shirt, those muscles eye me with suspicion.

"Are you a faggot, Raulito?"

"No."

My mother will be back from work soon, the checkerboard floor is going to turn into a sea of parallel lines, I sense it but am afraid of what those lines will tell me, so I look my brother in the eye. Even though his eyes are filled not with love, but with terror. My brother looks at me, horrified, as if I were not a person but a snake with a hundred heads.

"If our old man finds out, he'll kill you, and he'll get thrown out of the party, and maybe even out of work. It's forbidden to have a child who is homosexual. Give me the women's clothing so I can throw it out right now. Come on, this is Mamá's fault. You think I don't know? You think I didn't see her pretending you were Nancy . . . ? Mamá really messed you up. She turned you into *this*."

To my brother, I am "this," which he indicates with the tip of his finger, I'm the unnamable, Raulito the Spineless is now Raulito the Shadowless, but when I go out at night, I'm Wendy, and I meet young men who treat me like a very sweet girl, a slip of a thing, a young woman who won't let anyone touch her between the legs because she's a virgin. Like the waves of the sea before the sun has come up, that very pretty girl is a virgin, although anyone can kiss her, anyone can press his lips against hers, his tongue against her tongue, drinking in her saliva, because she allows it, she's a bit easy, that girl, but she looks European, she seems French or German.

My brother enters my room and looks for the women's clothing, but the clothes are not in my room, I'm not that stupid, my friend and I hid the clothes in an old abandoned house where no one lives anymore, we keep a box with our clothes and our makeup there, we're so careful, we go in when nobody's watching, and we only go out if the dog we give scraps to isn't barking. The dog's name is Alicia and the house is called Wonderland and it's on the other side of the mirror.

If I could go back to Cienfuegos, my Zeus, I would go back to that house that is falling apart by the day and everything would be the same again, but the Erinyes are flying over my head already and they persist in their chanting.

It's unraveling, it's unraveling, it's unraveling! the Erinyes sing in their raucous voices, and over there in far-off Cienfuegos, my dog Alicia, who still lives in Wonderland, begins to bark inconsolably. I don't have much time left, I know, because the words of the dark-skinned lieutenant, whose role in the Cuban army is the same as that of Hermes on Olympus, are resounding in the ears of the captain.

"Was I right?"

"Of course you were right in coming to tell me," the captain says at last. "That's what friends are for."

I'm not a friend of the captain's, I was the container into which the captain poured his anguish, nostalgia, and semen. Now I'm the pebble in his shoe, I'm not even worth reading the worn-out letter he keeps in his pocket.

"His good name depends on your silence," Apollo whispers in my ear.

I'm invisible. Not even Carlos scolds me when I lag behind in formation.

One afternoon, after we receive the day's orders, Agustín advises me to desert.

"Where would I go?"

"I don't know, but get out of here. If they ask where you are, I'll say you went to the infirmary—I don't know, I'll think of something. They're going to hurt you, Raúl, if you don't leave . . . The captain is losing his mind. Just leave."

My father set a crab free. He let it walk around the middle of
the living room that my mother had cleaned so diligently.
It got the checkerboard floor all sandy and looked at us with its
pincers upright, it seemed happy, as if its destiny were different
from that of its siblings: the big pot full of boiling water. I'm five
years old and my father has left a crab wandering loose so that my
brother and I will calm down. Both of us sitting in the rocking
chair, we watch it move back and forth, as if asking itself what
is this place, this new planet it came to in a bag, surrounded by
friends who are no longer there. The crab is alone in the middle
of the living room, it's alive, but it's already dead, because soon
my father will come for him. A sad fate for a crustacean, who at
least has his pincers to pantomime a defense.

have my AK, the captain is going to call me, he's going to carefully touch my feet and will whisper to me to leave my quarters, that we have to talk. Everyone pretends to be asleep, even Agustín will pretend he's sleeping. Then he'll take me to the bush, and I won't return.

I think back to that photo of all of us, from just after we arrived in Angola. I have the newspaper in my hand, I'm sitting in the infirmary while the nurse is looking at me with a smile as enigmatic as the Mona Lisa's. The nurse has my right foot in his hand and he says that my skin is as smooth as my complexion, which is the prettiest thing about me. He whispers it, because there are other soldiers listening. They have just one year left before they go back to Cuba, the ones who are going back. I'm not going back. I feel the nurse's hand on my foot and imagine the photo from when we just arrived in Angola and I look like a little toy soldier and everything is gray around us. The nurse kisses my feet, I feel the dampness on my soles, then on my ankle.

"Girl's feet," he says, "not a single hair."

Then he'll close the infirmary and think of me, and also a little bit about the captain. He knows the captain and I are doomed.

The nurse knows the rumor is like an avalanche of tanks advancing and that it's already being discussed among the division's top officials. That's why he said what he said, because he knows there's no way out of this one for me.

"Too many pieces are at play here. It's hard to simplify in life, not like in chess," says Agustín, who sits facing me, playing chess. He sacrifices his queen to declare a checkmate that later ends up being false, and the game ends in a draw.

"I miss the sea," Agustín says. "When I go back to Cienfuegos, I'll go to Rancho Luna and spend a month there without getting out of the water."

"There's not much time left," I tell him, and he says nothing will happen, that sometimes things seem more terrible than they are, that I shouldn't be scared.

"I know, but I'm scared all the same."

"You shouldn't have come."

"I came because of that extra inch."

"Nothing will happen to you. I don't think they'll hurt you."

"Why would they hurt me?"

"I don't know," Agustín says, because there are things you don't talk about, it's something in the air, like the ghost of the leopard, like the whirlwind of the dead, like the Erinyes who chant over my head that ditty about unraveling. I almost bring my hands to my ears to keep from hearing them, but I don't do it. I know them so well, ever since my time in Ilios, they've surrounded me with their wiry locks, with their eyes coming out of their sockets, with that impatient smile that lacks even a hint of joy. I'm also surrounded by the dead warriors, Martínez, and the South African I killed.

On Friday, after receiving our orders, it's the day for cleaning weapons. I grab my AK, I take it apart, clean it with gasoline, and begin to oil it. I've named it, it's called Cassandra, just like me, because the butt is made from light-colored wood, almost blond. The soldiers from my company sing while they take apart and clean their weapons. They sing a song to the tune of Gardel, inserting the words *I knew he could fit an artillery cannon, four tanks, and a German army railcar in his ass.* The voice that stands out the most is Johnny the Rocker's, a high-pitched voice that gives into a strange tenor timbre like a leaping dolphin. Then they move on to *I'm leaving your country*, and they finish with that part that goes *goodbye, lady, / goodbye forever, goodbye.*

I'm listening to them from here, Zeus, from the earth where I lie, dust among the dust. That corrido has been with me since we were getting ready to disembark in Angola. It was our true national anthem. We sang it when we were able to score some rum or high-proof alcohol, and if we couldn't score, we sang it, and now, under the African sun, when we are already aware of what it means to be at war, what it is to shiver feverishly with a thirst that won't go away, what it is to carry fear the size of an enormous house, we sing it now too. All so that when we least expect it, Johnny can suddenly begin to hum, then to whistle that one about Hotel California, pretending that he's an American rock star and we're his fans.

"Marilyn Monroe, come on and dance!" yells Martínez, who is still alive and who forgets he's an officer when he drinks and mixes with the soldiers.

"Recruit Raúl Iriarte, alias Marilyn Monroe, get out here and dance Hollywood style, so as to further the education of these airheads assembled here," orders Lieutenant Martínez, who has a degree in journalism and is in charge of the battalion's political education.

I've also had too much to drink, I've had the two drinks Agustín gave me with a smile and, given my scant height of five foot one and the fact that I'm barely a hundred pounds soaking wet, I go to the middle of the room, very close to where Johnny the Rocker is, I close my eyes and move with languor, but my dance has very little to do with the Marilyns of this world, I move like my sisters and I danced when, along with our mother, we paid tribute to Hecate, the dark goddess of the moon. I move and pat my now invisible heavy breasts with hands adorned by bracelets that are also invisible, I smell the meat being offered up, I see the other women's feet and their anklets. I'm a princess among other princesses while the Rocker sings "Hotel California" and we're all drunk, except for the other officers, who traveled to Luanda.

To leave the battalion in the hands of the Miramar dandy is to hand it over to the void, to perdition. Martínez and Sergeant Carlos give orders when no one else is there, and the first order is to go to the nearest village, get some aguardiente, and drink until we pass out. For the aguardiente, we trade cans of Russian meat and Spam, that oily, damp pig pulp that tastes like sleepless nights. I dance as the Rocker sings "Hotel California," but when he's about to start a Beatles song, Sergeant Carlos, who has tired of Johnny's made-up English, which sounds something like "*chuotell cayiforlnia, yustinaue usi yustinau usi,*" says, "That's enough. You're making my brain hurt with that little song. Let's have a conga."

Carlos starts beating his palms and several others start to tap on the crates that used to contain rifles, and then Agustín's voice breaks through the sad Angolan night.

"*King Kong, King Kong / te persigue un batallón*," Agustín sings, and it's as if all of us were that giant monkey in love, chased by the New York police from skyscraper to skyscraper.

"*King Kong, King Kong / te persigue un batallón!*"

I'm singing with Agustín and the others, my Zeus, and suddenly I realize that I'm happy and that I would be happier if there was nothing else, if we remained fixed on the canvas of your memory forever, if we never, ever moved again, but when Agustín finishes, Martínez says he sings like Bola de Nieve, that he should have never come here to waste his talent, and then Agustín breaks into that one about *Vete de mí* and the impromptu musicians stop playing on the AK boxes and the Angolan women halt the *tam tam* with which they grind the cassava, and monkeys and birds stop their shrieking in the trees and the leopard's steps become more cautious.

"*Tú que llenas todo de alegría y juventud / Y ves fantasmas en la noche de trasluz . . .*" Agustín sings without looking anywhere in particular and Cuba returns from where it never should have gone and it enters Angola and we all have so much to think about, my Zeus, so much.

'm ten years old, I'm reading "The Pit and the Pendulum," sitting on the sidewalk in front of my school, waiting for the bell to go in. Nearby is the bust of José Martí that no one has cleaned yet, so it's soiled with dust and almond tree leaves. I'm wearing a pair of sandals that the Russian woman gave my father to give to me. The sandals are a light chestnut color and are too feminine for Cuban tastes. Because of these sandals, one of my classmates will yell at me, "Little girl!" I have the book open on my knees and suddenly a man comes over to me, I sense him dragging the leaves with his feet. When he's in front of me, his shadow sneaks over me, I finally lift my head and before me is an individual in an old-style suit and a strange hat, with a tormented look on his face, he speaks to me in a language I don't understand. Those eyes that shine like fire in a very pale face, so out of place in the tropics, they're what stands out about him. I look into his eyes and the school disappears. The man holds out a hand and, when I grab it, I feel something cold run through my veins, something I can't name. Then he takes the book, looks at it closely, and pages through it. His entire ensemble, his entire figure, they give off an air of something antiquated and archaic, something I don't know, although I've read a lot about it, and that something is death. I sense it in this man of medium height who stands before me while the children play at recess, running, taking that soft drink they give us for a snack along with two pastries each. No one sees the man, the man is invisible to everyone else. He's an "apparition," I think, because I've heard that word said by my mother and by my aunt Nancy, the one who looks so much like me. There is a silence around the two of us, no one approaches to invite me to play, no one notices the man, who returns the book to me and, with a gesture, asks me to stand up and follow him. We leave the schoolyard, we walk along the corridor toward the exit, but when we're about to go out the wide door, someone puts a hand on my shoulder.

"Where are you going, child?" she says, and when I turn around, I see the Spanish teacher looking at me with eyes wide in alarm.

"I'm going with him," I say, but when I look again, the man is no longer there.

I didn't tell anyone, but years later, in one of those youth cultural magazines, I saw a picture of the man who appeared to me and realized it was Edgar Allan Poe. He was the first dead person I saw, I saw him before I was Cassandra, I saw him before the gods who later came one by one like those big drops that precede a hurricane. Now I'm in Angola and the dead surround me, they beat over our heads, they slow down all our movements, all our motions, so that we come to a stop like toys whose pull cords have run out, and we can't take another step, we remain fixed in place, and our actions superimpose themselves on each other, and the captain tells me his good name depends on my silence at the same time as the Black lieutenant asks him if he was right. The declaration and the question remain suspended in the air with a very deliberate kind of suspense, Zeus Pantokrator of everything and nothing. I could tell the captain, "Give me peace" and then my death would have some trace of dignity, I wouldn't just be a recruit dragged into the night to die the way leopards and hyenas die. I could tell him that and then the captain wouldn't feel obliged to tell me, "I brought you here so we could talk, Raúl, because we have so much to discuss. You told everyone, and I can't allow that."

I didn't have to tell him, "I didn't tell anyone," I didn't have to tell him, I should have kept silent, but behind me was the goddess Athena, suggesting responses, and I was looking the captain in the eye and I knew that in just a few minutes, the AK was going to do the talking, I knew that the bullets would crash into my body while in the battalion, in the division, in the Cuban army, everyone was sleeping, even the sentinels were sleeping. Agustín, lying in his hammock, so close to mine, was sleeping, having forgotten the promise he made to my father that he was going to protect me. What I returned to the Old World for is already happening, the captain already wants me to kneel down, to be wretched, so that I don't remind him so much of his wife who died in Cuba, and I kneel down and I'm wretched and I ask him not to shoot me, please, that I didn't tell anyone nor will I tell anyone, I stretch my hands out before him, and I beg him, "No, my captain, I'll do whatever you want, no, my captain."

"You mocked what I loved most," he says and finally lifts his AK and points it at my blue eyes. "And scum like you has to be wiped off the map. You sabotaged a man's morale in combat, you took everything away from me, Rauli, everything."

Now that I'm no longer around, my mother hangs Nancy's favorite dress over the back of a chair and maintains infinite dialogues with her sister, she tells her all about me, that I'm in Angola and that I've grown over there, I'm almost six foot five and I've also sprouted muscles and learned English, French, and Portuguese, and I'm going to return married to a very Black princess with a thin waist and she's going to accept her because you have to indulge your children, Nancy, so they don't leave, like José, who is now in Miami, ninety miles away, and no one knows how he's doing.

"If I had given an inch when he showed up here with that little Black dancer, things would be different now," my mother continues, rocking in her chair, facing the navy blue dress that Nancy's ghost inhabits.

"I watched the fall arrive, / I heard the sea singing, but you weren't there," my mother sings with her honey-sweet voice, she sings while she knits a wool hat for the daughter I'll have with my Angolan princess, she knits while on Radio Progreso they announce "your twelve o'clock *novela*," she sings while I am about to die.

N o one knows that the captain has brought me here to kill me, everyone knows that the captain has brought me here to kill me, all of those young soldiers and sergeants who admired him so much know that he brought me here to kill me, all of those officers from the battalion's leadership who play baseball with him, who drink rum with him, who scratch their balls along with him, they know that tonight is my night, that Marilyn Monroe will cease to be a problem, they sense it.

"I can't let this go. You played with my name," the captain says and shoots.

The captain shoots, the bullets go through me and I fall sideways like a keeling ship, I start dying slowly and I feel like asking him to forgive me because he's watching me die the way you would look at a wounded animal, he kneels before me and wants to tell me he's sorry and he acts as if he's crying, but he can't cry, my death doesn't matter at all to him although he wants it to matter so he doesn't feel so dead inside, no one will come to see about the noise of the shots, no one. It's normal to hear shots in the African night. I feel myself ceasing to breathe, I feel the Erinyes calling me, they hold out their hands and keep whispering,

It's unraveling, it's unraveling, it's unraveling, it's unraveling. I'm slowly dying while the captain looks at me. Later, he'll take me to the training camp and will bury me in the same hole that I dug as a punishment. He'll do it because he feels guilty about not having killed me before. He'll take that risk. But no one will see him, or no one will want to see him.

"What happened to Marilyn Monroe? Did she desert?" my sergeant Carlos will ask the next day when he confirms that I'm not in formation.

"He probably overslept," Johnny the Rocker will say.

You're looking at a piece of wood on the shore, a tiny piece of wood you found amid the stones, there where the beach becomes wilder, you keep looking at that piece of wood on which there is an inscription in a language that takes you to other times, and then that piece of wood is so old that it's impossible for it to remain in your hands and it starts to grow, to take on a wavy shape, to become something else and you become something else along with the wood and you're sitting on the shores of a sea that is not Cuban and behind you is the city and you are also someone else, you're finally Cassandra, and in a few minutes, they're going to call you by your winged name.

"Come," they'll say to you, "come, run over here, the vessels are approaching, leave that old statue of Hecate that the priests abandoned, come over to Poseidon's temple, come and we'll sing those songs we love, Cassandra, come."

A NOTE ABOUT THE AUTHOR

Marcial Gala is a novelist, a poet, and an architect from Cuba. He won the Pinos Nuevos Prize for best short story in 1999. His novel *The Black Cathedral* received the Premio de la Crítica Literaria and the Alejo Carpentier Award in 2012 and was published in English by FSG in 2020. Gala also won the 2018 Ñ Prize of the City of Buenos Aires–Clarín for *Call Me Cassandra*. He lives in Buenos Aires and Cienfuegos.

A NOTE ABOUT THE TRANSLATOR

Anna Kushner, the daughter of Cuban exiles, was born in Philadelphia and has been traveling to Cuba since 1999. In addition to *The Black Cathedral* and *Call Me Cassandra*, she has translated the novels of Norberto Fuentes, Leonardo Padura, Guillermo Rosales, and Gonçalo M. Tavares, as well as two collections of nonfiction by Mario Vargas Llosa.